BIG LOVE

C000247244

BIG LOVE

By BALLA

Translated by Julia and Peter Sherwood

JANTAR PUBLISHING

London 2019

First published in Great Britain in 2019 by
Jantar Publishing Ltd
www.jantarpublishing.com

First published in 2015 in Bratislava as *Veľká láska*

A CIP catalogue record for this book is available from the British Library
ISBN 978-0-9934467-8-8

This book was published with the financial support from SLOLIA, Centre for
Information on Literature in Bratislava.

LITERÁRNE
INFORMAČNÉ
CENTRUM

CONTENTS

INTRODUCTION

BALLA'S BiG LOVE

Long overshadowed by Czech literature, its partner from the former Czechoslovakia, Slovak literature has rarely been available in translation, to say nothing of making an impact on international readers. Almost 25 years after Slovakia attained independence as a state, however, its writers are finally appearing on the global scene, with several new English translations, including the contemporary fiction anthology *Into the Spotlight*, published in the last few years. Of these, among the most significant are two books by the award-winning postmodernist Balla: the current volume *Big Love* and his previous collection *In the Name of the Father* (2017). Both were published by Jantar and translated by Julia Sherwood, who works in collaboration with her husband Peter and has been almost singlehandedly responsible for the recent emergence of Slovak literature from near-total obscurity.

Slovak critics have compared Balla (who does not use his first name, Vladimír, in his literary work) to Kafka. While this seems to be the default comparison for much of Central European fiction, it is justified in Balla's case not only by his absurdist edge but by his daytime career as a bureaucrat. His native town of Nové Zámky hardly seems a rival to Kafka's mystical Prague, yet with its substantial Hungarian minority, it is one of the most ethnically diverse corners of the former Czechoslovakia. The self-enclosed nature of his texts, beginning with his first book of short stories, *Leptokaria* (1996), is heightened by his frequent use of intertextuality. His mainly autobiographical protagonists are trapped in their existential isolation and unable to communicate with an absurd world, as reflected in the title of his second book, *Outsiders* (*Outsideria*, 1997). Despite the alienation that pervades his work (or perhaps partly because of it) Balla is firmly established as one of his generation's leading voices in Slovak fiction: he was given the Anasoft Litera prize, Slovakia's leading literary award, for the novella *In the Name of the Father* (*V mene otca*) in 2012, and *Big Love* (*Veľká láska*) was among the ten shortlisted finalists in 2016. While the central thread of the present narrative involves the relationship between Andrič (a pitilessly semi-autobiographical character like most of Balla's protagonists) and his girlfriend Laura, *Big Love* is primarily a critique of contemporary society, in which the triumph of liberal democracy has increased rather than diminished the Kafkaesque aspects of life. Andrič's friend and colleague Panza is afraid to criticize their office even when walking on a mountain path: 'an experienced bureaucrat won't let himself be deprived of totalitarianism so easily and carries it with him wherever he goes... [he is] convinced that you must be scared in a very sophisticated way, whereas in the old days you could be scared openly and 'officially', so to speak, fear was something that was officially accepted, sanctioned, and went without saying...' When Andrič first meets Laura, she is wearing a neck brace as the result of a car accident, while he himself is in a constant state of 'preventive fear', reflecting the mass paranoia and dissatisfaction that has settled into European and world politics in recent years.

The ethnically mixed setting of Balla's stories reflects the historical issue of national identity whose ramifications continue into the present. With no independent kingdom in the past, Slovaks faced the existential struggle of defining themselves against linguistic and political assimilation. Under Hungarian rule before World War I, minority nationalities were repressed, and after Czechoslovakia was established, the dominant Czechs often looked with condescension at the smaller nation's desire for autonomy, which was achieved by the creation of a wartime Slovak state. Under Communism, the tensions between the Czechs and Slovaks were submerged beneath socialist brotherhood, but as Martin Votruba has noted: 'Mutual comprehension was achieved through the country's bilingual media, which alternated the two languages conscientiously, but Slovaks and Czechs never learned to speak each other's language.' The return of democracy after 1989 led to the division of the shared republic in 1993 and conflicts with Hungary over language and citizenship issues. The central metaphor of *In the Name of the Father* is the bizarre house built by the narrator's brother, whose underground labyrinth represents not only the family but the nation. Yet as the narrator observes, 'This town's inhabitants had nothing in common with any kind of nation.' Much of *Big Love* takes place in the Tatra Mountains, but in one scene Andrič returns to his hometown in southern Slovakia and encounters a group of nationalists in a bar. Late at night, the last one to remain gives the protagonist a long monologue that could be characterized as 'Make Slovakia Great Again', praising the fascist leaders of the past and announcing: 'We've united with all the nationalists in the world, except the Ukrainians! Even the Hungarians! ... But what would be best of all is if everyone loved the Slovaks. That's what I call big love, no question about that. But for starters it would help if everyone respected their own leader. A leader must love his nation more than anyone else does and lead it against other nations.' It is telling that the first appearance of the eponymous phrase 'big love' has no connection to Andrič and Laura, but reflects the resurgence of xenophobic and authoritarian trends that many people hoped had been left in the past.

Despite the freedom and relative prosperity brought by the post-Communist reunification of Europe, life has lost any deeper meaning for many, including 'the insecure and confused bureaucrat Andrič', who 'argues with his client about whether he is in fact a client or not.' While many of the references to political and cultural figures are specifically aimed at Slovak readers, the general feeling of inertia and ennui goes far beyond the Central European context. Yet Balla's deconstruction of current reality reflects the specific experience of post-socialism, in which many longstanding assumptions were broken apart, including the elevated role of the writer. Before the existence of independent states, national identity was rooted in language, which was protected and nurtured by the writer, so the age of national revivals in the 19th century gave writers pride of place in Central and East European societies. Under the Communist system, the writer was seen as the 'engineer of human souls', still playing the nation-building role but now in the service of ideology. Even those who became disenchanted with Communism served the nation through their dissident activity by opposing the regime. But the lofty role of the writer came tumbling down after the revolutions of 1989: without the shared excitement of smuggling hidden messages past the censors, literature lost much of its appeal (and readership) in post-socialist Central Europe. The generation of Slovak writers who came of age in the last decade of the twentieth century, which includes Balla, was the first that could truly pursue 'art for art's sake', free of political or social demands, but in an atmosphere of aggressive materialism, it remains an open question whether literature retains any role at all. *Big Love* addresses this issue through the conversations between Andrič and Laura's mother Elvíra, who (as the narrator ironically notes) 'had once lived with a writer who was in some way similar to Andrič, except he was talented.' Although her flat is still filled with books, Elvíra dismisses Slovak writers as a reflection of their nation's 'semi--conscious' existence: 'they all lack patience and perseverance', she tells Andrič: 'In fact they lack everything a good writer should possess, but above all they lack experience. Experience with women, apart from anything else.' While formerly a teacher of Slovak literature, Elvíra admits, 'Eventually I became so disgusted with Slovak writers that I switched to teaching Russian literature... Fortunately writers don't exist anymore. Because to exist is to mean something.' Nonetheless, the novel is filled with references (both affectionate and ironic) to real-life Slovak writers (as well as Czech, Hungarian, and Polish ones) and even to Balla's publisher, the indefatigable Koloman Kertész Bagala, who appears unexpectedly at a bar in Rotterdam: 'This man looks perfectly at home wherever he is, as if he belongs wherever he happens to be... Dishevelled, unkempt, unshaven, frustrated, on the brink of bankruptcy and madness – but right where he belongs.' Andrič himself, like all of Balla's protagonists, never finds this sense of belonging.

The loss of social significance for the writer found its symbolic expression in an obsession with sexual impotence, which became such a prevalent theme for younger Slovak writers in the 1990s that the British doyen of Slovak studies, Robert Pynsent, dubbed them the "Genitalists", a group he characterized through their 'ironisation of male genitalia and an explicit concern in their fiction with modern Theory, especially French varieties.' While the Genitalist label was never fully embraced by Slovak critics, Rajendra Chitnis employs it in his book *Literature in Post-communist Russia and Eastern Europe*, which includes what is probably the best analysis of Balla available to the English reader. According to Chitnis, Balla's *Leptokaria* "transforms sexual impotence from a condition of weakness into an ideal state for the writer, the endless promise of creation that is never fully realized." It is not surprising that in the opening scene of *In the Name of the Father*, the narrator finds himself in a doctor's office 'with my tool hanging down and my balls in the doctor's hands.' The examining physician orders him, 'Don't ever procreate because you will father a predator.' In *Big Love* (which similarly opens in an examining room) Andrič's impotence manifests itself through his paranoia, even while urinating he reflects obsessively about the potential of artificial intelligence to eliminate human life: 'he was confused, he was missing something, something to do with his tool, you can't cheat nature, he thought to himself, while the world kept spinning.' Andrič considers himself 'a responsible parent' precisely because he has no children, but his refusal to have them is probably one of the factors that ultimately dooms his relationship with Laura (who is already a single mother and initially claims not to want another child). He loses his 'big love' due to his unwillingness to change with the circumstances: 'Such a change was something they both feared, although it gradually became clear that, in fact, he was the only one who feared it. It could have meant, among other things, that he was satisfied with his life as it was. Or rather: that he had resigned himself to it – one shouldn't mistake resignation for satisfaction.'

Balla's fiction seems to offer little comfort to the reader, except for the grim pleasure of confronting reality in its true emptiness. Yet the author insists that his intention goes beyond the mere exploration of despair. In the introduction to an excerpt from *Big Love* published in the anthology *Into the Spotlight*, Balla comments: 'I've been writing to appeal precisely to those people who share my strange perception of life, and this helps to create the kind of community that is able to survive in a world that feels quite alien to them.' It is in this search for meaning, hopeless though it may be, that Balla evokes the older, quasi-sacred role of the writer in society. However, his community is not that of traditional religion or the nation (Slovak, Hungarian, or otherwise), but those outsiders, misfits, and lonely souls who are unable to identify with these or any other categories – a group, he suggests, that is much larger than we might think.

Charles Sabatos
Istanbul, January 2018

[Parts of this introduction were originally published by the *LA Review of Books* in August 2017 under the title *The Slovak Kafka: On Balla's 'In the Name of the Father.'*]

BiG LOVE

Outside the door of his office, he blacked out.

The doctor stated it was nothing but a minor indisposition.

Why and when these things happen, no one knows.

By chance?

He gave the doctor a dejected look:

'I think I am being remotely controlled. I can't quite put it into words, they don't want me to put it into words. They can switch me on and off at will and it's quite possible that when they next switch me off they won't switch me back on again. Sometimes we aren't even aware of being controlled by an outside force, I'm not always aware of it myself, but I won't be conned by the fact that I'm not aware of it! As long as they have some use for my mind, they'll keep sending their instructions but then, at some point they'll turn off the switch, and you will call it Alzheimer's, or dementia, or whatever. The body that belonged to the mind will be disposed of, there are rituals for that. Traditions! Listen, doctor, I saw this film yesterday, it's called *Stoker* and there's this scene in it, for some reason it's set in a kitchen, and the main character is reading *The Encyclopedia of Funeral Rites*. Quite a useful read, don't you think?'

The doctor patted him on the back:

'You say you're being manipulated but in fact you're just dying to be manipulated. You're frightened of the void you might plummet into once you realise there's no one above you. How desperately we all wish there was someone above us! Just to prove that atheism is a great big humbug! We bend over backwards to present fear and delusions as a virtue, as a manisfestation of humility, respect for tradition, authentic knowledge. God, Bach, Protestantism, Catholicism, virtues, stuff and nonsense, all of it!'

'But they really are using me. And not just my mind. Whenever they feel like it, they remove my organs and send them to Albania. Or rather, to Kosovo. That is why our government doesn't recognise Kosovo. It's trying to protect me. It's doing everything it can. The government is concerned about all my component parts, such as my liver, but has to keep it secret because of international legal protocols, that's why press conferences sometimes give the impression that our Prime Minister is a bad man, but in fact he's good, he's protecting me as a citizen, if you see what I mean!'

'Let's do some tests, shall we? I'll call the nurse. Then we can start you on medication.'

The first time he saw Laura, she had just been in a car accident and was still in shock and in a neck brace for whiplash. He, on the other hand, spent all his life in a state of shock and permanently in a condition of preventive fear: once he made the doctors put his leg in traction before it was even broken; another time he stood in the street making weird movements, extending his arms and bending forward, then flexing his elbow as if drawing something towards him as he bent lower and lower, and lifted his left leg at the same time, until he fell over, repeating this several times until a neighbour, who was watching him from the garden – there's always someone watching you – asked what he was playing at.

'A colleague is coming to pick me up in his car. I'm practising opening the door to make sure I don't get hurt as I get in.'

My neighbour got the point and has since started chemotherapy and pre-op tests although he has yet to be diagnosed with any illness.

A sceptic must always be prepared.

'll pull up here,' said the man at the wheel, 'by the gate.'

The gate opened onto a small courtyard, behind which there was another gate and behind that, a path leading to the asphalt road to the hotel.

Andrič, in the back seat, was feeling his ankle.

Suddenly he pierced his skin with a fingernail.

He didn't know whether he did it on purpose – it just happened.

A wound opened up and started bleeding but all he could feel was a strange kind of chill, as if grass was about to sprout from there, its tiny roots already itching under the skin.

He stopped attending to his foot and concentrated on the driver's broad face: he was listening to something his daughter Laura was telling him, and didn't like what he was hearing. For some unfathomable reason, she was explaining to him that these days children are no longer called after their parents, that young people always rebel against ancestors who assigned them names according to tradition, naming son after father, daughter after mother, that this was how they tried to liberate themselves from their parents: they wanted to be fully independent and this was one way of taking a stand. Laura's father got her drift: after all, she didn't name her little girl after herself either, and by doing so she had distanced herself from her father as well, in a way.

'Oh, I see!' he fumed, banging the steering wheel with his fist. 'But I'm good enough to chauffeur you around, am I?'

'It's taking a stand, but not a perfect stand,' Andrič chipped in. 'It would be perfect only if young people refused to have children altogether. But since they don't refuse, for of all their protestations they are exactly like their parents, who also had children. You should find that reassuring,' he said, egging the driver on. 'None of this messing about with names is genuine rebellion! Children should be left completely nameless. Christian names and surnames connect us to people we don't want to be connected with. Christian names and surnames have become tarnished by our parents, they're millstones around our necks. And to cap it all, there's also baptism! Mind you, there are some who practically fall in love with their parents, but those are pathological cases.'

He got out, said goodbye to Laura and her father, and started walking around Starý Smokovec, which was in the grip of a typical Smokovec winter. He was a regular at the station bar. The wooden shack was surprisingly cosy even though it had no tables or chairs, just tall counters. He suddenly felt the urge to get to know one of the patrons, whose thick sweater appealed to him.

'You must be a skier,' he said to break the ice.

But the conversation didn't get very far because it turned out that the gentleman was German, which triggered unpleasant associations for Andrič, since Laura's ex-husband came from Bamberg. In addition, Andrič didn't feel like speaking German so instead he just stood at the bar, thinking, or rather, just allowing certain images to float to the surface: Laura and her daughter on a sledge, Laura and her daughter building a snowman, Laura and her daughter taking a ski lift.

To sum up, the little girl enjoyed a lovely snow-bound childhood.

When he was growing up in the Lowlands – he found this term for the plains of southern Slovakia repellent, it must have been coined in the Uplands, a term he found equally repellent – when he was a child down south, the snow would barely reach up to his four-year-old knees. The memory of his childhood knees brought to mind his paternal grandmother. There's a photo that shows him wading through the snows of south Slovakia, aged four, with a tiny old woman dressed in black from head to toe. She reminded him of a crow but he loved her very much, despite a hate campaign waged by his mother. She wanted him to hate his paternal grandmother and save all his affections for his other grandmother, that is, her own mother, though she wasn't particularly fond of her either, because her own father, Andrič's grandfather, had waged a campaign against her. Andrič was very fond of his maternal grandmother, too, perhaps even more than of the little black crow, since his father didn't agitate against her as intensely as his mother agitated against his paternal grandmother; Andrič was also very fond of his agitating grandfather – his mother's father: as a child he obviously had plenty of affection to spread around. It was only when he grew up and developed a sufficiently vicious and cynical way of thinking that he started to see his father's mother as a small black crow – such a thing would never have occurred to him earlier, as to his child's mind crows were always enormous and terribly dangerous.

The German in the jumper made him think of Laura's Chinese story. Not long ago she'd been to China with her German husband and fell in love with Shanghai, but on her return one of her husband's friends, a deranged, racist socio-logist, tried to convince her that the Chinese were intent on taking over the world as part of a long-term secret plan, and that the Chinese regime didn't represent capitalism, socialism, feudalism or slavery but was rather a living organism bent on global expansion with the aim of preserving its genetic stock.

'Minute fragments of this supra-individual creature are all around us, the deranged sociologist told me,' Laura later explained to Andrič, 'ostensibly selling cheap trash or junk food in restaurants, or sometimes kidnapping women and children to use as ingredients in tinned meat, but in actual fact they are only carrying out the plans of an organism that has no plans, being the plan in and of itself, like the ants on the windowsill of a Balatonfüred restaurant, mind you, I didn't get the thing about lake Balaton from that sociologist, it's something that happened to you and me, you may recall,' – no, he didn't – 'how the ants all laid siege to a potato chip, then a column of them lifted it up and carried it to the antheap instead of gobbling it up selfishly in an orgy of instant, short-term gratification, as that would have meant that only those individuals who happened to be closest to the bait, or rather the chip, could have satisfied their hunger, while they are, in fact, controlled by some higher organism, an ant-being of a higher order, I'm sure that will remind you of Rudolf Steiner's teachings,' – no, it didn't – 'the conscious or unconscious goal-directedness of the ant collective militates against the individualistic ant, although in this particular narra-tive the ants are not ants, the ants here are the Japanese, I mean the Chinese, which means they have attained a level higher than we have, because what is at stake is the survival of the genes, the survival of the ant-principle, although the ant, I must stress, is not an ant, I think the Russians would also like to attain a higher level but no good will come of that, that's something the Russian organism has long been trying to do, but all it has achieved is the elimination of millions of Russian individuals, nothing nobler or more progressive, except that it is precisely those eliminated individuals who have bequeathed us the profundity of Russian literature with its profound Russian souls, my bookshelves at home are full of it, so who knows how it will all end with the ants, I mean the Japanese, I mean the Chinese, but the rest of us are just mindlessly devouring our future, of which it is certain that neither we nor our children will form a part,' she concluded and Andrič had to admit that the Chinese may yet give us serious pause, although normally he couldn't stand women pontificating. He wasn't keen on men pontificating either. In this respect men are just women camouflaged by muscle and bodily hair. Fortunately, Laura wasn't on the whole inclined to pontificate, she was too busy raising her daughter and trying to find her a new father.

This is one of the forms self-sacrifice can take.

Everything for the child's sake.

Who could object to that?

Poliačik, a member of the Slovak parliament, once said that raising a child is the greatest miracle of all. In fact, he had taken part in a sacred shamanic ceremony. He might have saved himself the trouble and could have immediately impregnated a woman and got on with raising his offspring, that would have given him his greatest miracle. But I guess Poliačik wouldn't have been happy to follow such a straightforward path to happiness, or perhaps one that didn't involve participating in a shamanic ceremony, he would have had too many doubts about his happiness and maybe, if he hadn't first tried out the shamanic path, he would have ruined everything, without shamanism his happiness would have been shaky and constantly undermined, and that is why he did the right thing.

Let us render unto Poliačik the things that are Poliačik's.

Andrič, too, was attracted to shamanism, provided it didn't involve a perilous journey to Peru. He would gladly have been initiated and woken up in his own tiny flat. But he wouldn't have said no to real love either. For example – although this is by no means essential – love between a man and a woman. Between him and Laura. That would have been a conventional thing to do, it had been done a million times: it would have been far more original to steal a fire engine or to break into a church using a broomstick, or to hijack an aircraft while the pilot was using the toilet.

After downing a few beers with some agreeable strangers in the Smokovec bar, he met up with Laura again, who now had her daughter in tow, and soon all three of them were bent double as they dragged a sledge along a snow-covered road, Laura was laughing and so was he, although his laughter was rather strained, as he was running out of puff. He thought he might collapse into the snow any moment and let go of the cord, allowing the sledge to hurtle down the hill dragging Laura with it, but fortunately the hill wasn't steep, it was only he who was unfit and to make matters worse, he was wearing trainers which immediately became sodden through with water sloshing about in them, especially the shoe that was full of holes, his wet socks kept slipping down his feet, scrunching up in the toes of his trainers and beginning to make them feel too tight, the smile on his face was rapidly turning into a grimace, and since he was wheezing, it was just as well that he wasn't expected to talk, as Laura's daughter was doing all the talking, telling some magical children's story set in a magical children's world and featuring animals that popped up in her narrative willy-nilly, inspired by those they saw on their walk: ducks, a shivering cat and the crows were all incorporated into her plot. The little girl kept sinking her hands into the snow, which made pulling the sledge more difficult but Andrič didn't blame her, recalling the little Andrič he had been many years ago, that is to say, he forgave the child because by doing so he forgave himself for a second time, and while he certainly possessed a certain degree of empathy, had he once not been a child himself, he would never have understood Laura's daughter, but on the other hand his memory was poor and he remembered very little of his own childhood, except the things he sometimes managed to recall when looking at faded photographs, so his understanding for this child amounted to zero and with this zero degree of empathy he was now, in fact, growling rather than laughing and kept turning round again and again to see what was going on and what shenanigans the child was up to on the sledge: just at that moment she was planting her boots into the snow trying to plough furrows in it, without appreciating how seriously this impeded the movement of the primitive vehicle, although the young Andrič hadn't realised either how much more difficult he was making it for his father to pull the sledge by similarly ploughing furrows in the snow, and maybe it was while his son was ploughing furrows in the snow that the first sign of anger crossed his father's face. The little girl was digging her boots into the snow with whoops of joy, that's the kind of thing children do, they dig their boots into the snow and whoop, Andrič realised, gasping for breath and on the verge of total collapse as he trudged on alongside a bright and cheerful Laura. Laura was in her element: mountains, winter, snowstorm – for Andrič the light snow just starting to fall amounted to a snowstorm – in all this Laura was in her element, but then again, was there anywhere that this spirited young woman wasn't in her element? After all, most people enjoy nature, in winter, summer, and especially spring, although autumn isn't to be sniffed at either. Laura longed for a seaside holiday, as the sea is the epitome of nature, its very essence, and Laura was very keen to take her daughter to the seaside, and the little one was naturally up for anything that was fun, including a trip to the seaside, obviously somewhere south, not north, whereas the only seaside trip Andrič would have found tolerable would have been to the north, Poland or Germany, or even better, Sweden or Finland, places where none of them could go swimming and therefore there would be no danger of drowning and of consequent problems with transporting the dead bodies back to the motherland – provided, of course, the corpses were found in the sea to begin with – there would definitely not have been any danger of drowning in the north, where they would only go for walks along the coast and watch the cold surf from a safe distance, and could later chat about the cold surf and the shivering seagulls on the horizon over a nice cup of tea or a mug of grog in a well-heated hotel room. But the trouble was, Laura longed for the sea. Nature in the far north is cold and dying, whereas in the south it is bursting with life. Laura regarded any talk of well-heated hotel rooms as perverse, one should long for sunshine not for heating, sunshine was natural and heating was perverse.

Later in the evening, after their walk with the sledge and the long trek back into town, she suddenly announced, out of the blue, that in her view men were not really aware of most things or events, but simply made them up, relying on misinterpreted allusions and superficial observations, but that was no way to understand the way of the world and the rules that govern it, and those who didn't understand the basic rules would fail at the basics, such as raising children. She was obviously hinting at something. He was so offended that he stopped talking to her, sat down between the speakers and put on a Giacinto Scelsi record. When she despondently asked him what he was doing, he said he was listening to Scelsi and doing so out of sheer rage because he could listen to Scelsi only when he was in that state of mind, and he had been waiting for this opportunity for a long time. But as he was explaining this at great length, suddenly feeling grateful to her for making it possible for him to listen to the music, his rage evaporated and from that moment he was no longer able to listen to Scelsi, which embittered him so much that he went on listening anyway, suspecting that he could have gone on like this until morning, and the longer he went on the more he was hurting and tormenting Laura who was still despondently waiting for him in bed, which made the tension so thick you could have cut it with a knife and that, in turn, enabled him to steep himself ever more deeply in Scelsi's music, thus enabling him to put this evening down as an unqualified success and forget about Laura's thought-provoking remark.

Three months later drops of water were glinting on the wooden tables of the hotel terrace, every drop reflecting an image of Panza who was assiduously wiping down part of a bench, repeatedly testing the cleaned section with the palm of his hand and being dissatisfied with the result.

'Still damp,' he muttered to himself.

He shook his head and kept tapping the wood and sniffing his hands to check if it was excreting something smelly and sticky, because everything that is smelly and sticky is disgusting.

'When I was younger I used to get turned on by a woman's whatchamacallit, upper arms. Weren't you?' he asked Andrič. 'You know, rounded, brownish. That bit from from the shoulders down. But touching an arm like that won't get you anywhere. So what's the point of making all that effort, huh?' he added, and continued to attend to the damp bench with an offended look. 'You might make contact with beauty, dear colleague, you might touch it, but it's no use. Beauty will still be beauty and you will still be hideous. Unless you get turned on by your own arms. The reason I'm satisfied with myself is that I no longer wish to change anything about myself. But I don't want to take early retirement either. Who could live on 300 euros? I might as well hang on to the office job. I just hope there won't be another political revolution. Or an election.'

Andrič sipped his Fernet, burying himself in his memories as in a soft eiderdown. One layer of memories covered the next.

The Veronika layer was covered by the Marika layer, beneath that lay the Diana layer, somewhat further down lurked Martina and so on, ad infinitum, right down to mitochondrial Eve.

'All right, a woman was missing from your life so you took up with the lovely Laura,' Panza reasoned. 'You've given up your independence. I've been independent ever since I left the Movement for a Democratic Slovakia. They disappointed me. They did nothing for me, and I got nothing out of them. I'm just a bureaucrat but at least I got where I am by myself, without pulling any strings, by sheer hard slog. The Movement was still a gleam in their founders' eyes when I was already shuffling papers from one desk to another! And here I am, still at it. At my age! With my health problems! Yes, that's right, you've given up your independence. I'm not even sure it's been worth it. That's what women do to normal people. But then again, since when have you been normal? Someone like you isn't normal, you won't last very long. Anyway, isn't it nice here by the lake? Boats bobbing on the water. Oh, look, there's a chap fallen out of a boat. As I've said, it's nice here. Just as well I didn't tell my sister I was going on an outing. She might have wanted to come along. But what would she do here? She would just sit here badmouthing everyone. She doesn't like the water. I told her I was going on a training course. She'd never strip down to a, watchamacallit, bikini, swimming gear. But of course, I wouldn't either. I mean, why would I show off my hairy whatsit here?'

He stirred his coffee, grasping the cup.

A gob of spit flew over the railing into the water.

'If only we always had a view like this. That's what I call a sight to behold! Women hikers, young mothers, the waitress! Mind

28

you, I'm no longer interested in women. Only in the chicken in my courtyard, and my little pooch. But the pooch has died on me. I'll have to get a hardier one next time. By the way, I swiped some soap from the office the other day, a few bars in a nice blue wrapper, heard anything about that? No? That's a relief, then. So nobody's noticed. I can use the soap at home. We get through a lot these days. My nephew has refurbished our bathroom, I really enjoy going in there now, for a wash or a shower. My sister and I take turns in the bathroom. It's always occupied. We have to knock on the door. We keep knocking all the time. I don't know what she gets up to in there. Though I really have nothing against my sister. In the evenings I keep her company in the kitchen, drink some vodka, you can't smell that on your breath as much as gin. Although there's nobody I need to keep it from. My sister drinks too. Every day after work I pop into the supermarket and buy a bottle. Just a small one. We're not alcoholics, after all! And some beer. We don't spend that much on booze, I squander a lot more on heating. But we'll manage somehow, we'll survive.'

He stirred his coffee, grasping the cup.

'My dear fellow, why don't you give your Laura a nice present? You could cut a beetle in two and paint both halves some nice bright colour. It will make a beautiful and appropriate gift for people of refined taste. They love original gifts like that. Although sometimes it's not enough and they are still dissatisfied and dejected. Maybe you should make her a whole bunch of beetles cut in half, say half a dozen. You can pick up loads of them over there in the meadow, they'll leap straight into your briefcase of their own accord. Look how many I've got already!'

The first time Andrič saw Laura her neck was in a plaster cast. He realised it would be hard to get at her artery but that wasn't how he made his mark on women: what he took aim at was their vulnerable minds.

That was his métier.

The vulnerable female mind with its easily predictable strategems.

Apparently, he underestimated women.

That hadn't always been the case though: there was a time when he would fawn upon them, both literally and metaphorically, like the men in Bruno Schulz's drawings.

Sometimes it worked, sometimes it didn't.

When it worked, the memory of his initial fawning made him hate the woman later.

When it didn't work, he hated her from the outset and remembered her forever.

What was Laura wearing on that first day?

A light summer dress or perhaps a winter coat?

He wasn't sure about anything except the plaster cast.

She was standing outside a bookshop in the square, the one next to the café that has since closed down – everything that's good closes down, everything that's bad is proliferating – perhaps her slender upper arms existed only in his imagination, as he can't have seen them if she had worn a winter coat, but if he wasn't imagining them, she must have been wearing a light dress. A young woman in a light, pale summer dress, with a sad smile directed at her little daughter, who was either scampering about on the sun-drenched pavement or was cradled in her mother's arms so that her bootees didn't get wet in the snow.

Laura with her green eyes gazing into the distance, or at him. He stood on an elevated spot not far from the bookshop while Laura strolled in a depression in front of the café. In fact, she couldn't have seen him, as she was short-sighted and her narrow, gold-rimmed glasses didn't help much, especially given they happened to be stowed away in her handbag since they would have been useless amid the heavy snow that was falling.

Later, he came to learn that Laura came from a good family and had never brought shame on it, even when she had a car accident taking a sharp bend in the mountains from which she escaped with injuries to her neck and spine. The little girl didn't come to any harm that Slovak doctors in a Slovak hospital were able to detect. The accident happened because she was preoccupied with the thousand things she had to do, the execution of grandiose plans, and dealing with a number of minor problems. The fact that she was constantly busy and exhausted, always short of time, and naturally, as a result, distracted, provided further evidence that she was a valuable human being who belonged somewhere, who had found her place in life where she was called upon to tackle the various tasks and overcome the obstacles that inevitably crop up in the functioning world of intelligent creatures.

He, on the other hand, did nothing but constantly expect some event or news to drag him into the current of life.

To stop him from loitering on the margins.

It could have been a text message, for example.

Or an e-mail.

But it could just as easily have been a letter marked private and confidential, something of great import that would help assimilate him into the well-oiled machinery of the globe, into a human story with twists and turns and a cathartic ending, the kind of story the writer Staviarsky was telling him on their way to their hotel after a night out drinking somewhere in Poland, or was it when they were headed from the hotel for a night out drinking somewhere in Poland?

Except that after that night on the tiles he forgot the story and it became Staviarsky's.

She lay with her back turned to him.

He could feel her warmth.

She could feel the bulge of his belly.

The light from a street lamp illuminated their faces and every pimple on them.

Bad diet, stress, not enough liquids.

That might apply to anyone.

Their value on the vast market place of bodies was depreciating.

People die, animals die, plants die, hope dies, there's no point haggling over it, there's nobody to haggle with. End of story.

Andrič kept repeating the phrase *end of story*, while Panza muttered the word *hope* as if they were shuffling empty egg shells.

Andrič leaned over to Panza:

'They buried Juhász yesterday. We were at school together. I wouldn't say I liked him but we would meet from time to time. If I dislike someone, I avoid him, steer clear of him, but still find it reassuring to know that he's alive somewhere. Has he moved abroad? All the better. But when I hear that he's died, it's a wake-up call. Like being punched in the face. Even when it's a scumbag who's died, it wakes me up. And it's the waking up that matters, my dear fellow.'

Having said that, he dozed off for half an hour.

He awoke to Panza's words:

'We're in the European Union, right?'

'We are.'

'And Spain is also in the EU, right?'

'It is.'

'I was wondering if I could text my nephew. He's gone on holiday to Spain, with his wife, of course. Their daughter stayed behind, she'll go some other time.'

Andrič started reading an essay on structuralism because he didn't know that the whole point of the structuralists was making sure nobody should read them. After a while he replied:

'You need to activate something to send texts abroad.'

'But that happens automatically these days.'

Andrič's structuralist sentences fell apart.

Panza went on:

'Yesterday I texted my nephew and instantly got a message from the system that the text had been delivered. But I don't believe it! It wouldn't be the first time he didn't get a text.'

'If your nephew didn't reply, it means he didn't get your text. But you can never be sure. Maybe he just doesn't give a damn about you.'

'You think so? He's always been a bit of a bastard, that's for sure.'

'So you're saying he hasn't replied?'

Panza turned to look at the waitress and said over his shoulder:

'No, I'm not. He did reply. But I still have my doubts. It's always more sensible to have doubts.'

Laura's daughter drew a picture and went out to the court-yard to show it to the dog. The dog belonged to the owner of the guesthouse. A van was parked by the gate, and next to it was a motorcycle with leather seats. The child kept feeling the seat with her fingers, caressing it lovingly. Some white fluff drifted down from the trees onto the petrol tank, which sported a geometrically accurate drawing of a pentagram.

Andrič was sitting in the hotel room in front of his laptop, hoping that he had a secret mission in this world. He didn't have enough strength to believe that his life didn't have a mission. If he were physically strong he could carry bags of cement up to the fifth floor and wouldn't have to pretend to be a writer. So he sat there waiting for a winged messenger to arrive with a specific task for him, a clearly defined goal in life, but if one were to come Andrič wouldn't believe that his wings were real and that his halo hadn't been generated in post-production.

Besides, the visitor might have got the wrong floor.

Andrič had already sent two previous ones packing.

Too many tragic mistakes of every kind have occurred in the course of history, people exerting themselves in vain, dying for values and ideals, marching across continents, murdering and letting themselves be murdered, only for it to transpire later that they had been deceived or had deceived themselves. But peacetime isn't free of snares either – the insecure and confused bureaucrat Andrič often fails to deal with his client's business because instead of following procedures, he argues with his client about whether he is in fact a client or not.

Are they even in the right office?

Having an argument exhausts both of them far more than dealing with run-of-the-mill official business.

But what if Andrič was not meant to deal with clients?

Maybe he was meant to spy on them.

Maybe he was meant to incite them to rebel against the powers-that-be and take matters into their own hands.

A parallel secret government has established a parallel secret institution with the outward appearance of being part of the state apparatus, but for the express purpose of inciting the citizenry, awakening their thirst for blood and their proclivity for terror and total destruction.

On the other hand, it's quite possible that the only purpose of the entity that inspired Andrič's doubts was to confuse him so that he, in turn, would confuse as many others as possible. That would be something worthy of the devil: not just to divert people's attention from their true calling but turn them into his assistants to boot.

He had had intimate relations with other women, before he met Laura.

There was even one into whose eyes he gazed for a long time.

This happened in a café in the square.

He decided to tell her what bothered him, what was on his mind, that he was brimming with subjective impressions and universal truths and that was why he couldn't be a poet, he confided to her what plans he'd had in the past and that he no longer had any, since long-term, concentrated thinking brought about inaction, but were he still planning anything, it would have been a life with a woman just like her and in order to achieve that he was willing to reassess all his previously held beliefs.

The woman fixed him with a basilisk stare.

In the end she swallowed him whole and when she finished digesting him she swallowed another man.

He never stopped loving this woman.

Roaming the streets were freezing, half-dead winos, who had been out in the cold since forgetting to return home after the night before. A homeless man had wet himself and now stood shivering on the steps of an Asian bistro.

Andrič, on his way back from Laura's, was in high spirits.

He returned to his home town and in the early hours wandered into a gambling den where a bunch of nationalists were sitting at the bar.

He got a fright.

To camouflage his fear, he exclaimed:

'The next round's on me! What will you have, gentlemen?'

They sniggered at the Alibernet stains on his shirt. But the stains were also proof that he meant his offer. To convince them he produced his office ID and passed around his wallet stuffed with banknotes. This caused such astonishment among the nationalists that the wallet eventually ended up in his pocket safely and with its contents intact.

However, soon after that he fell asleep with his head on the counter.

When he woke up he noticed that only one nationalist remained.

The man started talking:

'Our grandfathers were great men. Nothing would stand in their way. And that's precisely what made them great. Great Slovaks, great men, great National Party supporters! They did some foul things, some dirty things, too, sometimes it was Slovak against Slovak, which is a shame but sometimes you have no choice when you're cleaning a pigsty. You know Šaňo Mach? For God, for the nation!'

With that he gave the sleepy Andrič a mighty slap on the back of his head.

'You see, now I can tell my wife that last night I gave a bureaucrat a drubbing. I've lived a full life! And one more thing: if our leader doesn't win the presidential election, the only thing this nation deserves is to be screwed. But I'm not worried. He is going to win! Either everyone is like us or, if they're not, they are at least scared of us. Nobody dares say a word, they all back away when we march down the streets and have a go at them. It's quite a mystical experience. Makes you feel you're growing taller. They're just a pile of shit, you get my meaning? They're all either frightened of us or agree with us. There's no one for us to defeat. We've united with all the nationalists in the world, except the Ukrainians! Even the Hungarians! You know how many nationalists there are in Hungary? That's what I call a nation! Even though we hate each other like poison! But respect, fuck it, respect! Hats off! But what would be best of all is if everyone loved the Slovaks. That's what I call big love, no question about that. But for starters it would help if everyone respected their own leader. A leader must love his nation more than anyone else does and lead it against other nations. Like Orbán and whatshisface … you know, the one we've got. Although sometimes he's as slippery as a snake, so I don't know what to make of him. The other guy, the one who founded our republic, he really had balls! And let me tell you one thing for free: the only source of national values is tension. Conflict, pure and simple. It's the only thing worth living for, that and giving someone a good hiding!'

The next time Andrič woke up he was alone at the table.

iles of children's books, toys, a car with a working electric engine, dolls with long flaxen hair entangled in the bars of an ornate kitschy cradle lay on the floor of the guesthouse, and by the window in one of the rooms stood a big bed covered with a floral duvet.

That's where they lay down and did it for a while.

Andrič wasn't used to prolonged and inventive lovemaking, nor did Laura try to impose this kind of novelty on him, she didn't say a word, just breathed heavily, and occasionally the rhythm of her breathing would become irregular.

Then they washed themselves in the tiny bathroom.

First one, then the other.

They looked at themselves in the mirror and smiled.

First one, then the other.

He at himself.

She at herself.

anza lives with his sister, and people at the office have been whispering about the siblings' private lives. But not everyone has to have a private life and not everyone has to be intimate with everyone else. When his colleagues learned that Panza's sister had a little moustache sprouting under her nose and that she was quite burly, some confusion arose: maybe she wasn't his sister?

Was Panza sleeping with his own brother?

He hadn't shown any real interest in women for a long time. Sometimes when he and Andrič went for a shot of gin to a café regularly frequented by young businesswomen, a furious Panza would get up as soon as they arrived and make a dash for the toilet.

'Keep an eye on my coat and briefcase!' he said emphatically, 'this place is swarming with sluts!'

Andrič had the impression that Panza's sister provided him with everything he needed. By this he didn't mean sex because he was sure that Panza didn't need any. A person who needs sex will make at least a token effort in this direction, for example by trying to dress stylishly so as not to repel potential partners, but Panza had been wearing the same jumper, the same polka-dot tie and the same terylene trousers for years.

People who dress like that might as well forget about sex.

Andrič had met his sister once. It was a few months ago, when Panza invited him to a fête in his home village.

He arrived by bus, found Panza's house and rang the bell. Nothing happened for a long time, then he noticed the curtains twitch at one of the windows and made out a round head of a female with a round male head behind it.

The heads were watching him.

He rang the bell again.

This time he kept his finger on it for nearly a minute.

A window opened, a woman with a thin moustache leaned out and asked amiably who he was looking for. When he answered, she said:

'My brother's gone to the cemetery.'

'The cemetery? But he was supposed to be waiting for me. I'm a colleague of his. I'll go and find him – where's the cemetery?'

'We have two cemeteries. One new and one old. They're at the opposite ends of the village.'

'So which one did he go to?'

At that moment he saw Panza dart behind his sister's back.

'Our mother is buried in the old one, and our father in the new one,' Panza's sister went on. 'And my brother usually just says he's off to the cemetery, but he really goes to the co-op or the baker's. Nobody can tell in advance where he'll go. You can wait for him in the pub across the road if you like.'

'When is he coming back?'

'I don't know if he's coming back. Sometimes he stays the night at his nephew's. That would be my son. There's a village fête on, you see.'

Andrič sat in the pub for about thirty minutes.

Then Panza turned up.

'My sister told you a pack of lies. I'm sorry, but that's what she's like,' he said, making a strange face.

'What kind of lies did she tell me?'

'I was at home, when you rang the bell. I was having a shave.'

'No matter,' Andrič said with a dismissive wave, but couldn't help raising an eyebrow at Panza's three-day stubble.

Just when you need to find someone in town who's off his head so you don't feel you're alone, there's suddenly no one around.

But in the privacy of their own homes people get up to the weirdest things.

The other day he heard his neighbour howling on the other side of the wall like a rutting deer.

The howling went on for an incredibly long time.

It sounded as if he were being skinned alive.

But suddenly, to his amazement, he realised that his neighbour was howling with pleasure.

He also overheard the repeated sighs of a timid female.

Surely they weren't making love?

After years of marriage!

That surprised him because he always made sure he kept women at arm's length, even at the most passionate stage of a relationship. He failed to notice that the women were upset by such detachment. They became depressed and felt they weren't sufficiently attractive. They would lock themselves in the bathroom at night to inspect their bodies and would often find that at certain times of the year the buttocks under scrutiny were far from perfect.

At night he tended to be asleep and had no idea they did this.

During the day he and Laura would leaf through books that demanded the greatest possible concentration and a great deal of time. They collected books of this kind, money no object, and fooled themselves into thinking that they would study them in detail later, when they were together for good, rather than sporadically as now, when they met only once or twice a month in hotels and guesthouses. Then they would have a proper discussion about what they'd read. They planned to foster their intellectual development jointly, though they knew that intellectual development was a joke.

They should have focused on stealing, not on development.

But they assigned greater value to development, almost out of spite.

Stunned booksellers often told them that no one else bought the kind of books they did, they were dead stock.

They would take their purchases to cafés but once there, they would watch young people instead of reading.

As he watched others Andrić also kept Laura under constant watch.

By now he was convinced that watching was his true mission in life and wouldn't have minded making a deal with the devil: he thought he would be able to watch the devil, too, without suffering the consequences.

However, when it came to Laura, he should have loved her instead of watching her, but he was merely curious; he thought that curiosity was love and big curiosity was big love.

I n the early evening he went to the pub again.

Somebody was yelling:

'Čarnogurský is spying for the Vatican! He deserves to be shot, the bastard! His brother has privatised Váhostav! And you all just sit here and have no idea that eight metres under ground there are concrete reinforcements, I swear! They are fifty kilometres wide down there, you can't even put a figure on it. I've spent all my life working hard and all I have to show for it is an old record player while someone has all this stuff underground! And we're sitting here and haven't a clue, just look at us, just drinking beer! And those crafty editors-in-chief! They live off our money, our pensions! But nobody writes about that. I've been a communist all my life, paid my dues faithfully, so in the old days I was entitled to ask the chairman of the district council if he really was a party member and what was he up to with this socialism of ours. What kind of communist are you? I asked him straight out. None of your business, he said. You're the last person who should talk to me like that. You're the ones who have screwed everything up! Filler, his name was. My father-in-law was best man at his church wedding. A communist who had a church wedding! With a priest and the whole shebang. You know the sort. When this council chairman died he was whisked away by helicopter. Even though helicopters didn't even exist then! By the way: who's paying the artists? How come they can even graduate from that academy of theirs?

You know, the music one. Let Čarnogurský pay them, but not out of my pension! And he wanted to be President? All right, he's a national socialist, and so was his daddy, I'm fine with that, but what about later? When he was against Mečiar?! I'm not falling for that anymore!'

Andrič was sitting far away from everyone else, including his own friends.

By now he knew all their topics of conversation and how their utterances depended entirely on the so-called independent media – that's why they increasingly tended to talk rubbish. When he was on his own, at least he didn't have to worry about the expression on his face: it didn't have to be either sad or happy, either aggressive or meek, either focused or distracted: his face hung on him like a wet sock from a washing line. But the new pub generation took a different approach to their expressions: instead of unwinding behind poker faces, the young men and women deliberately and provocatively used it to rub everyone else's face in it. Their discarded masks and expressionless faces spoke a straightforward, vulgar language, and the unguided missiles of their vacuous visages punched Andrič like clenched fists right in the place where he usually wore his face in a focused and disciplined way, although even when that happened, the light in his eyes would suddenly go out at the most inopportune moment.

He returned home beaten to a pulp, even though no one had touched him.

n the early evening he took off for the pub again.

Someone whispered:

'Just look at that guy. He defected to Sweden in '68. He knew something about economics, made a fortune. After '93 he came back and went to see the prime minister Mečiar, and said that as a patriot he had some advice for him on economic matters. Mečiar didn't give him a job but gave him a reference for another. And this bloke then went and used Swedish money to privatise every single business that could have competed with the Swedes and shut them all down. That actually happened. The engineering companies were in competition with Husqvarna, so they were shut down. Kysucké Nové Mesto, the bearings factory. Shut down. We were just starting up in the drilling business, wanting to compete with Sweden and hey presto: we had to shut down. And so we did. That's what happened. Is that what you call democracy?'

'Well, isn't it?'

'But what does this tell you about the system?'

'How do you mean?'

'I mean, what does this tell you as a Slovak? I'll tell you what: democracy is not when the Swedish economy is working, it's when the Slovak economy is working.'

L aura's mother Elvíra was an ethereal being not just in terms of her femininity but, above all, in a kind of angelic way. Andrič expected her one day to float up into the air before him, and even apologise for doing so with a sad smile, then immediately sink back down to the floor and admit that she found flying depressing but she couldn't help it.

That's how her life has turned out.

Well, what can I say.

From time to time she levitates, believe it or not.

In a tower block, on the fifth floor in fact.

In a small room surrounded by shelves full of Russian classics.

On a dark bookshelf beneath them rested the giants of Slovak literature, including those who have come to be regarded as giants solely because in our neck of the woods there's a shortage of genuine giants.

It's good that there are backwaters where nonentities can also be regarded as major figures.

If Elvíra suddenly dropped to the floor, if the angelic magic stopped working all of a sudden, she would shatter into a thousand tiny shards like something made of precious glass.

He was worried for her.

Sometimes she was so pale!

He was also worried for Laura.

And for her little girl, too.

But mostly for himself.

On his visits to the flat Elvíra shared with Laura and her daughter he grew temporarily fond of his name, with its mellifluous Slavonic sound.

Laura also uttered it while they were having dinner in a shepherd's hut in the Tatras.

The fire crackled in the fireplace, snow glittered outside.

The waitress heard his name and she gave a sharp look.

He blushed.

As if her hand had touched him down there!

Sipping his 52% alcohol slivovitz, he noted that she was wearing a folk dress and eyed her carefully. After a few shots he had difficulty telling the difference between the leatherette back of the chair across the table and the screen of his laptop, and waited for the website of the most widely read opposition daily to load. In the meantime he showed Laura's daughter his I.D., explaining what the individual items of personal data on it meant.

'Why don't hermaphrodites have intercourse?' he turned to Laura with the rhetorical question.

'Because they don't feel envious of anyone or anything,' he informed her without waiting for an answer. 'They don't feel the need to possess anyone or anything, they already have it all. Hermaphrodites don't need someone else's beauty. Being smooth and rounded they don't seek the hirsute and angular as their antithesis, and being soft they aren't fascinated by another's hardness.'

After that he just sat there.

Something inside him was broken.

He had seized up.

Slowly, one at a time, drops of sweat slid down his forehead onto his eyebrows, some getting stuck there, others slipping lower down and pushing on into his eyes. He reflected on the fact that these days computers take decisions about everything, even about computers, and that Stephen Hawking has warned that the best computers will soon surpass humans in intelligence and develop even better computers that will surpass and eliminate every previous generation of computers but, above all, will permanently and brutally eliminate human beings, yet people are still barely aware of this danger, not planning any counterattack or taking any countermeasures, they just go to the toilet, wasting time on biologically conditioned acts that have them in their grip, just the way Andrič has grip of his tool above the urinal, and that reminded him of hermaphroditism again, he was confused, he was missing something, something to do with his tool, you can't cheat nature, he thought to himself, while the world kept spinning.

That night he didn't make Laura happy.

The following morning she pumped the accelerator up and down in agitation and the car kept making strange noises.

'If I can have a complete set menu for three euros, I'm certainly not spending twenty euros on lunch,' declared Panza from the back seat.

'You won't get prawns for three euros,' growled Laura.

'I'll make do with mashed potatoes.'

Their lunch in a wooden replica of an American ranch was served by a half-naked boy, and Andrič made a supreme effort not to look at anything in particular while Panza eyed the Székely cabbage passionately. After lunch they moved to the hotel terrace, where Laura unpacked the T-shirts and other items she had been selling to make ends meet since separating from her husband. There weren't many potential customers on the terrace, and on top of that a storm broke out moments later, boats were slamming into the pier but the noise was drowned out by the drumming of the rain. The wind rearranged and messed up the clothes Laura had spread out on a long low table and the strings of Indian bead necklaces seemed to rise up for a moment, reaching for the dark sky.

Soon hundreds of beads lay scattered on the terrace.

In the evening Laura's daughter made a tunnel out of mattresses, declaring it a cable car in the Tatras and started riding it from peak to peak, above the rocks, the moss and the mountain goats. The room in the guesthouse was illuminated by a red light, leaving the corners in the dark, and the child would later lie there in wait, emerging every now and then to whoop and jump around Andrič, hoping to attract his attention and his hugs.

But he just sat bent over his laptop trying to concentrate on his text.

The child began to seep into his text, virtually crowding into his lines.

The child turned into a line.

She turned a somersault and her legs kicked out as she laughed.

Laura lay across the double bed in her white panties, asleep.

Does she feel safe with him?

Is she not afraid for her daughter?

He felt a sudden surge of joy and continued to write, now with fresh energy.

A room, a woman, writing, life.

'I don't want any more children,' Laura said to him in the morning.

Andrič considered himself a responsible parent, because it is possible for someone who has no children to be a responsible parent, too: he starts by thinking about it long and hard, he carries out research, comes up with theories, is in two minds, gets together with someone and separates from someone else or else, if he doesn't sparate, he just goes to see a psychologist to sort things out, and in the end – in the end he has no children. Of course, he thought to himself, it's different for Laura: she is raising her daughter, she dotes on her, in this respect she is all sorted, she has no need for another child. That is why initially he couldn't understand the bitterness in her voice.

It took some time for it to dawn on him that she was desperate.

If someone had thrown him into the water at that moment, he wouldn't have started to swim.

He would have been swept along by the current like a piece of wood until he sank.

The fish, their eyes bulging, would have flashed past him fearlessly.

Do fish know fear?

What he knows is shame: he would have been ashamed to swim.

Swimming is a sign of one's instinct for self-preservation.

Would the Dalai Lama have swum?

Would the Buddha have swum?

Something terrible inside him answered: yes, they would.

So he was done with the Dalai Lama and Buddhism, but apart from that he didn't achieve anything.

He was standing in Laura's mother's room surrounded by books.

He sounded troubled as he recounted the dream he had the previous night. In fact, it wasn't even the worst dream he'd ever had: the slow-motion ones were the worst. In those he would be endlessly pedalling away on an old bike with small wheels, every turn of the pedals requiring a huge effort, yet he wouldn't be making any headway and was instead slowly sinking into some dark substance, so slowly that he would be aware, with exceptional clarity, of every single movement of his muscles and the coursing of the blood in his narrowing arteries and veins. He was sinking into the thick goo which formed bubbles that grew rounder and bigger before bursting. Behind him, in the sticky semi-liquid substance reminiscent of some bubbling asphalt of biological origin, he was losing sight of his father.

His father was frowning.

He watched him with his head turned back as he pushed the pedals.

They were both sinking deeper and deeper.

He made an enormous effort to imagine the face of this man, practically a stranger to him, wearing a different expression: after all, there was a time when his father could muster a more genial look, literally like a father who is, for some reason, happy to have a son, a wife, a family.

Andrič's powers of imagination were starting to fail him.

Elvíra watched him with love and understanding from behind the bookcases.

They started to talk about literature and Elvíra also brought up the fact that she had once lived with a writer who was in some way similar to Andrič, except that he was talented. He could let himself act, dream and write in a crazy way. People like this often ruin their wives' lives, in fact that was exactly what her ex- husband had done, though it was neither his obligation nor his intention, it was just how things had panned out.

Later the conversation turned on to capitalism and Andrič declared that what was killing him was not capitalism but people. They often claim they've had it with 'the abnormal' in art: they want to see normal films and read normal books, but nobody makes normal films anymore and nobody writes normal books anymore. And they blame that on capitalism. It's capitalism that turns people into monsters. People in the Czech Republic are angry with Petra Hůlová because of her novel *The Stepmother*, they say it's not a normal book and they are tired of all that.

But Andrič is tired of their tiredness.

If they're tired, they should take a nap on the sofa.

'They beat me up and left me for dead,' he said, returning to the trials and tribulations in his dream. 'I was lying in the grass, my mouth full of blood. My colleague's mouth was also full of blood, but not because he'd got a beating but because he'd coughed it up. He was dying of a disease that should have long been treatable but this treatment had not yet reached our neck of the woods. Only in my dream, of course. In reality in our neck of the woods no one is even planning to treat this disease.'

'I see. I recommend antidepressants. I couldn't last for a minute without antidepressants. Face another month? Year? Without antidepressants? Never.'

'Is there nothing else one can do about it?'

'That's the sort of question we used to ask under socialism. But it has turned out that it is this question that will live forever, and not Lenin.'

They should have a coffee.

What kinds of cofee-machines are there on the market?

Small lever-operated ones, automatic ones with an integral coffee grinder, machines that take capsules or pods, all you have to choose is a colour.

Brilliant!

'Let's have some coffee,' he suggested.

'Good idea. And some antidepressants. But first, a coffee and a cigarette. Those are the only things that keep me going. And it's really only in this sense that cigarettes and coffee are harmful.'

anza is sitting, listening to Andrič and nodding, or rather, he's not listening, only nodding, his eyes and his whole face make it clear that he doesn't understand, and how could he, since he's not listening, it's not that he is stupid, he just can't be bothered to listen, he's had bad experiences in the past when he used to listen and got nothing in return, so now he professionally and routinely doesn't listen, especially when a sentence begins in a complicated way.

Because how could such a sentence possibly end?

The assumed complexity of the ending puts him off listening, so all he does is sit there nodding and, strangely enough, the nodding doesn't give him a pain in his neck and besides, it's courteous to nod, so people talk and Panza nods.

When his friends are talking, Panza also smiles.

When his clients in the office are talking, he nods more slowly and smiles less because clients must be kept at arm's length.

This situation has become so routine for him that an uncomprehending, absent expression is the only one that is truly his, this is what makes Panza truly Panza and not just a Panza-mask.

He follows the sounds, using them for orientation like trail marks: ah, this is the beginning of a sentence, he ascertains from the intonation and the fact that before the sentence began there was silence, which he manages to recall with nostalgia for a fraction of a second, the beginning of a sentence is always followed by various things, Panza is on the alert for the sound of a full stop at the end of a sentence, because a full stop, too, has its own characteristic sound or rather, its own opposite of a sound, that's when you have to nod and then it's over, you can start talking about yourself, except that Andrič won't let him and just goes on holding forth, yet believes that he's holding forth not just for himself but also on Panza's behalf.

'Everything in our office is beginning to rot,' he says to Panza who, on hearing the word 'office', looks around in panic even though they are walking along a mountain path far from the hotel and no one can hear them.

Noticing Panza's panic makes Andrič aware of his own, because he too is scared, but now his fear has intensified, since it's out of the question for a bureaucrat with the ageing Panza's experience to be scared for no reason, it's more likely that the experienced bureaucrat hasn't allowed himself to be deceived by the illusion of freedom and the illusory turn to freedom that followed the collapse of the communist system. An experienced bureaucrat won't let himself be deprived of totalitarianism so easily and carries it with him wherever he goes, never stating anything openly and with no opinions of his own, convinced that you must be scared in a very sophisticated way, whereas in the old days you could be scared openly and 'officially', so to speak, fear was something that was officially accepted, sanctioned and went without saying, in the previous regime it would have been odd *not* to be scared, as even the officials at the very top were scared and they were in the best position to know that fear was justified because scheming was rampant, especially among those at the very top and indeed directed chiefly at those at the very top – the experienced Panza knows very well to what extent you had to be scared and how important it was to let your superiors know that you actually were scared – not in so many words, but in a covert, yet unambiguous way, while at the same time he imagined – and he wasn't the only one to imagine this in those days – that anyone might be his superior, including any passer-by in the street, you never know, he used to imagine, and treated every passer-by as his superior, just as he later began to treat as his superior every statue ideologically and theologically linked to Jesus on the cross, because after the fall of the totalitarian regime Panza automatically embraced another totalitarianism in the form of the Catholic Church, which is hardly surprising since in most people's minds totalitarianism is linked not only to fear but also to boundless hope and trust and the certainty that everything is, and will be, fine for evermore, totalitarian power not only metes out punishment but it also protects, and maintains the untenable, and so Panza genuflects before the chapels of the Holiest of Holy Trinities as well as the most garish, baroquely bloated sculptures and statues of the Virgin Mary and the infant Jesus, he crosses himself by the book, doffs his cap and bows his head, there is something studiedly slavish about this, it is normal, totalitarian behaviour, a cultural veneer; in other words, genuine subjugation. Panza knows that there is no way you can avoid bringing fear and servility out of the cupboard again or bringing it down from the attic, should you have been so rash as to have temporarily stowed it away, you have to dust it off and recast it pragmatically as unofficial fear and servility vis-à-vis the new power structures, having to render unto Caesar that which was once Caesar's and only after that can you render unto God what is left, because only whatever is left – and there mustn't be too much – can still be God's, but if anything is indeed left over, it must be His.

Andrič devoted more time to Panza than to Laura.

He always tried to integrate his current girlfriend into the circle of his closest friends, as if valuing her for the contribution she made to the collective, not for being his big love. His friends were welcome to take his girlfriends to the cinema or on days out, leaving him more time to be on his own.

Not every woman would put up with that.

As they walked around the hotel grounds Andrič forgot all about Laura and concentrated solely on Panza:

'I motivate my collective to get on with their work. But it's pointless and unfair. You might not be working very hard, but then again, why should you work harder? Your activity is as meaningless as most other activities. Your fate is at the mercy of outside forces, it depends on how the manipulated mob votes in elections. The mob is no longer manipulated by the idiotic media, these days it is manipulated by the idiotic views people post on idiotic internet forums. In this way sooner or later idiocy will prevail. No longer does anything depend on historians, political scientists, economists or sociologists. And the authoritarians who have failed to notice that the clouds are gathering and a thunderstorm is brewing, a storm of total dickheadedness, continue to scheme and plot to accumulate even more wealth than they have already, expecting that eventually, after their defeat in some future election – because there always comes the day when the winner of a previous election loses the next – will retire to the villas in upmarket neighbourhoods that they acquired by wheeling and dealing and there they will find a way to live out their days, dying in ideal circumstances of old age, because otherwise the deranged online revolutionaries will rip them apart with real – not online – teeth! For the moment the high and mighty are still under the impression that they will have the last laugh. Because who can their victims appeal to and where? To what authority? A revolutionary tribunal? Fine, but this tribunal will, in a totally senseless and chaotic way, make fucking mincemeat – excuse my language, my dear fellow, but fucking is the right word – it will make fucking mincemeat out of everyone! Of the high and mighty as well as their victims. For the time being all is calm. The other day I saw the villa of a local politician with sticky fingers. Colossal! For the time being! For the time being every city has its sticky-fingered politician neighbourhood. But once the fierce storm and monsoon rains arrive, the landslide will sweep them away like everyone else!'

'My needs are modest. I don't steal, I'm happy with just a bed, an eiderdown and some Turkish coffee,' mumbled the frustrated Panza.

'Idiocy is universal but at the same time it comes in all shapes and sizes and it's full of internal contradictions. So the members of the tribunal will sooner or later kill and consume one other. But first they will consume you,' Andrič went on unrelentingly, 'they will deprive you of that miserable little cubby-hole of yours and you won't even get a cup of coffee!'

Nature crackled and rustled beneath their city shoes.

Squirrels scampered about overhead.

'**Y**our belly is a trampoline,' said Laura, laughing.

This was a few months after they first met.

He was lying on his stomach feeling like an amorphous blob of jelly.

As she sat on top of him she was telling him about her plans for Saturday morning. She kept bending down to him rather too cheerfully, telling him that she was going to buy a book on positive thinking, she already had one which was very useful, it had helped her set herself some goals.

'You must set yourself one hundred and thirteen positive goals,' she declared, 'I have set myself nine so far.'

'Such as?'

'I want to have my hair cut. And I want a detached house and a cat.'

'We can't even afford a studio flat.'

'That's negative thinking. You have to change the way you think. You have to think that one day you will own a house with lots of rooms, with me and a cat and my little girl!'

'That's not going to work.'

'If it doesn't it will be only because you don't want it with all your being.'

'Including my belly?'

'You're making fun of me,' she said, bursting into tears.

He knew that in actual fact she had felt like crying ever since she woke up that morning.

She had long sensed that their relationship wasn't going anywhere.

He freed himself from under her in silence, got up and went out onto the balcony. The place was a mess, the concrete floor covered in rubbish, knick-knacks of every kind, wet underwear and crumpled shirts drying on the clothesline. He regarded it as a great achievement to have made it to work that day and to have managed to keep his admittedly rather bleary eyes open the whole time, to come home afterwards without, exceptionally, getting drunk on the way, and that later he even managed to tidy up a bit, not on the balcony, just in the flat, he didn't get around to the balcony but even this kind of partial tidying-up was a special occasion – he had done it because Laura was coming for a brief visit.

He was pleased he hadn't collapsed onto the bed after he finished tidying up although he did circle it a few times, even stopping by it once, but he managed to stay upright and had now made it to the balcony and only there did he realise that it would have been better to have got drunk after all since the outcome – Laura's tears – would have been the same either way.

A few weeks before their trip to the Tatras, Panza was sitting at his desk in the office, opposite Andrič. Panza was hunched over, plump, in a state of languid, lazy, siesta-like nonchalance, his too-short legs stuck in too-short trousers, his feet in large, seemingly smart shoes with the heels of their perversely thick soles resting on the lino.

The tips of his shoes made fitful semicircles in the air.

The other bureaucrats had already started streaming towards the exit of the office building, and proceeded from there down the single wide avenue of their small town to its shops, shopping centres, sports grounds, or in pursuit of sexual adventures or – in the case of the least fortunate ones – straight home.

Andrič leans towards Panza:

'Shall we go?'

Very slowly Panza looks around.

In fact he doesn't look around.

What he's doing is not looking around since he's not taking anything in, just turning his head. A curious, inward-looking smile plays on his lips, he is smiling at someone within himself, nodding almost imperceptibly, his eyes covered by a delicate film of pleasure, reflecting joy at his fully functional physique, especially his spine.

He is silent.

Andrič turns to him again:

'Shall we go?'

He knows that Panza heard him the first time, but that inspecting his body, and the subsequent relief he felt at the fact that certain of its risk-prone parts were operational, took priority over a response.

Panza now responds:

'I'm waiting for Habík.'

But momentarily he seems to be on edge.

Andrič presses on:

'Habík? When does he clock off?'

'I don't know.'

Andrič looks at the objects: two chairs, a desk and a typewriter, all museum pieces, just like every typewriter on every desk these days. A low table with a computer on it. A printer. A cabinet. Paper, paperclips, documents, boxes for blank forms, order forms for new boxes, notes and minutes concerning the shredding of documents, and preliminary materials relating to the planned shredding of notes and minutes.

Andrič looks at the objects and thinks of Laura.

They will meet again soon.

He is apprehensive whenever he is due to see her again after a break of two or three weeks: it's like getting acquainted anew, which could, in a way, be seen as an opportunity to make a fresh and better start every time, but to make the start different and better maybe they themselves should have, over those two or three weeks, become a little different and better. One reason why they always miss out on this opportunity, which is not really an opportunity, is that every time they see each other again, he feels less and less confident: her expectations of him are certain to have increased, whereas he keeps going back to square one, with no more courage and with plans no better thought-through than the last time, he can think of nothing better or more interesting to offer Laura and her daughter, having exhausted nearly all his good ideas and options the first time they met and ever since then it's been just a matter of repeating things. That's how he sees it, though Laura may well see it differently, except that he is not quite sure how grown women with children see things and what they actually see, he can't tell when they are bored and when they are having fun, when they are confident of having made the right choice at the outset and when they are beginning to consider taking radical steps.

The shadows in Panza's office have grown longer.

The sun is setting behind the cabinet and the unused safe, left over from the time the previous office had been abolished and replaced by the current one, which will, in its turn, be abolished before long, to be replaced by the next one, with a higher proportion of young, predatory relatives of the flabby old bureaucrats, alongside an ever-increasing number of young party members without shame or scruples, ready to jump on the bandwagon.

Nothing new under the setting sun.

Panza gets up, walks over to the window, rotates round his short axis and asks as he has a feel of the curtains:

'Did I close the window?'

'You did.'

'You'll be my witness if necessary.'

But he's still not convinced, he grips the window ledge pressing his bulbous nose against the glass and pushing hard to make sure the glass or the entire pane doesn't give way, and the curtains don't twitch in the approaching dusk that is falling upon the street. Ankles in grey socks sprout from his oversized shoes and disappear into the trousers flapping around his legs.

As if he were dancing.

He dances into the middle of the room and starts to twirl around again, tugging on his sleeves.

'Where is that fucking idiot?'

'What fucking idiot?'

It's not a real question, Andrič knows which one.

But why not ask?

'Habík! He's late!'

Panza pats the huge watch dangling from his wrist on a loose strap. Any abrupt movement makes his belt slide below his belly which is as loose as the strap on his wrist, so he grabs the belt abruptly and yanks it up his belly along with the trousers. He sits down again, assuming a spherical shape once more and stares at his shoes.

Eventually he resigns himself to the inevitable and gives up the fight.

He takes a deep breath, as if about to admit that the fight has indeed been lost.

Then he springs up, grabs his briefcase, opens it, checks its contents, and squeezes himself into his coat, ready to leave.

Andrič gets up too.

'But what about Habík?' he asks Panza.

'Habík is at home, in Podhájska. It's his day off. And so what? Can't he take a day off?!' exclaims Panza with the expression of someone who thinks Andrič is a complete idiot, on the evidence of his questions and his general behaviour.

At the same time he begins to feel sorry for the complete idiot.

And the capacity to feel sorry for someone – that's quite something!

His confidence grows.

In recent years confidence hasn't really been on his agenda.

That's why he now flashes Andrič a cheerful, waggish smile and exclaims with a gleam in his eye:

'Let's go! Don't just sit there! The beer's on me tonight!'

He grabs his briefcase, darts over to the window, gives it a tap: 'Did I really close it?' he turns to his colleague, wagging his index finger in front of his face in a joky, yet quite menacing way, stressing:

'You're my witness, if necessary!'

He hurries over to the door, and once there he looks back again, surveying all the useless objects in the useless office like a responsible boss, and exclaims: 'Come on, we're in a hurry!'

A few minutes later Andrič receives a call from Habík.

Habík asks why they didn't wait for him, he just got slightly held up switching off his office computer.

Andrič silently hands his mobile to Panza.

Laura's daughter is squealing.

Her fully functional vocal cords fill her with happiness, and her yummy mummy laughs because seeing her little girl happy makes her happy.

Andrič ponders the expression *'yummy mummy'*.

Try as he may, he can't imagine a decent person bearing this label. Surely no one, not even a child, could trust a mother who, rather than being a mother, is nowadays referred to as a 'yummy mummy'. 'Yummy mummies' tend to hang out with dubious young dads, characters who haven't yet managed to pick up a younger, better-looking or better-off woman but are already on the lookout for one. The expression 'yummy mummy' contains quite a bit of aggressive sexuality: while a 'yummy mummy' is indeed a mother, she is above all a young woman and yummy-mumminess suggests that the young mother is by no means averse to sex, that she is postmodern and even though she has no idea what the word means, she takes morality with a pinch of salt: after all, her child didn't come from a test tube, and where would you get so many test tubes anyway? A 'yummy mummy' is sexually active, she is a woman possessed of the full delectable arsenal implied by the term, publicly advertising her femininity through her child.

'You'll get a slap on on your tushie, you naughty girl!' her yummy mummy scolds her child gently.

Andrič promptly starts to ponder the word 'tushie' as well.

It is a word that is flippant while cunningly disguising its rather unsavoury essence: its inherent shittiness, its pong, its smudged grubbiness and, of course, a large dollop of sexuality. There was a time when he thought that the word referred to the vagina. He was mistaken. On the other hand, it's certain that when a yummy mummy refers to a child's 'tushie' in general, she is also slyly referring to her own substantial tush, which she craftily deploys to attract the male.

That's all well and good, but you can forget about the test tubes.

The tone in which the yummy mummy addresses her daughter is jolly in spite of the warning it conveys, her youngster's screams, attesting to the child's aggressiveness, audacity and groundedness, fill her with joy, as this demonstrates how completely the child has integrated into the present-day world, which favours the aggressive, the audacious and the grounded.

The yummy mummy's mind is befuddled by her daughter's happiness.

The little girl kept screaming, she had vocal cords so why shouldn't she scream: she was in tip-top shape, she had every right to scream, and even Andrič started to fall under the spell of the little girl's completely healthy screaming – surely this screaming was a good thing for him, just as he was a good thing for Laura, so why shouldn't he jump on the bandgwagon of such young healthfulness and take a walk on the sunny side of the street, for once!

Except that he was too self-conscious to hold hands with Laura.

It was even worse when she tried to embrace him.

His legs started to tremble and he couldn't help thinking that people were watching him and holding him accountable.

Is she not aware that relationships often break up?

That what we embrace today will be discarded tomorrow?

And that what will happen tomorrow is already brewing today?

He tripped on the kerb and let slip a profanity.

'You are drunk and vulgar,' said Laura bursting into tears.

But she continued to hold him firmly by the hand.

With her other hand she held firmly onto her daughter.

What matters is that the family is together, the thought flashed through his mind.

However, all his life he had suffered most when they were all together: the whole family, maybe not this family, as this is not yet a family, just an attempt at a family, the preparation for a family, in fact a kind of preparation that is itself at the preparatory stage.

Years ago, when he was still very young, he had no idea that everyone was just a victim of prevailing conditions, tradition, customs and the normality of the abnormal, and had no idea how much of a victim everyone was, and that everyone was at the same time a culprit, and just how much of a culprit everyone was. Only gradually did it begin to dawn on him that something was amiss, that there was some thing contorting him, constraining him, driving him into a corner, it wasn't just his parents but a thing of which his parents formed a part and that had turned his parents into an instrument of its will, driving them into a corner along with their child. This had marked Andrič for life and it is thus marked that he now stands by the kerb watching the tearful Laura, recalling the tense silence of a Sunday lunch thirty years ago.

The sound of cutlery scraping plates.

The radio playing softly on the sideboard.

What was on the radio?

What could have been on the radio thirty years ago?

That's exactly what was on.

You have to be very fond of your family if they are not to drive you mad one day.

You have to be very fond of something if it is not to drive you mad one day.

Two women on the train.

One says to the other:

'Is something the matter? I can see something's bothering you.'

'I'm in love with Andrič.'

'That's good, isn't it?'

'I don't know. I really don't.'

A long silence.

The other says:

'I don't know either.'

'What don't you know? Are you in love with someone, too?'

'Things aren't the way they used to be.'

A long silence.

The train stops, they make for the door.

One of the women says:

'Take care.'

'You too. It's just that...'

'What?'

'Andrič is crushing me.'

'You should crush him too. Sometimes that's the only point of a relationship.'

The Buddhist master expressed no opinion regarding what a student with lung disease should do.

A student so afflicted can't take deep breaths.

Nor can he exhale properly.

How is he to practise zazen meditation?

And is correct breathing the only way to liberation?

A sick body prevents you from escaping your own mortal coil.

The spirit in such a body will never vanquish it.

One day such a body will die before the spirit has even glimpsed its limitless depths.

But Laura's limbs are supple, her lungs are healthy, and she quite often sits cross-legged.

She enjoys using her body in this way.

She begins to take deep breaths and rises half a metre above the carpet.

Up in the air she collides with her mother Elvíra, who has been levitating for quite some time with a bashful smile.

They both come tumbling down to the floor.

Elvíra moves around the flat like a spirit.

She glides ethereally around the furniture, the books and especially the piles of clothes: in every room T-shirts, trousers, blouses, colourful jackets and underwear made in Asia are spilling from the wardrobes. The flat is packed to the ceiling, as it also serves as a storage place for the stuff Laura is trying to sell, with little success, though she won't give up because she never gives up on anything. This helps her to survive and maintain a degree of optimism, which her mother considers somewhat forced, the kind of optimism that often turns into a bout of hysterical sobbing at night.

And Elvíra? Her sadness is beyond words.

One night a bookshelf fell on her bed.

This was symbolic because the source of her sadness and melancholy was, most likely, reading and everything connected to it. But she also often mentioned how offensive she found the mentality of this country's populace these days. They're all sound asleep, not just when they are lying down but also when standing up, and also when sitting, walking, working, going out, getting married, getting divorced, and even when exercising their right to vote – they do everything in this strange stupor, this state of semi-consciousness.

A country of sleepwalkers!

A place ruled by hypnotists who take hypnotic pleasure in dominating their semi-conscious victims.

The people here are asleep, always and everywhere, they have no need of rebellion or revolution, all they need is torpor and hibernation. And if they do rebel or revolt it's only against the outcome of a previous rebellion or revolution that had unnerved them at some point, rousing them from their long years of sleep for a month or two.

'And as for Slovak writers,' Elvíra insisted over a cup of coffee on the balcony, 'they all lack patience and perseverance.'

This was a topic she raised quite often because it was constantly on her mind. Her last-but-one husband had been a writer and his tragic fate had aroused her interest in this issue.

'And of course, they are also uncultured and poorly informed.'

Andrič scanned the horizon from the balcony.

'In fact, they lack everything a good writer should possess,' she went on, 'but above all, they lack experience. Experience with women, apart from anything else. Mind you, I'm not talking only about male writers but also about female writers because they, too, lack experience with women, they don't know any real women. Reality – that's the tragedy. They don't know women and how they behave in tragic circumstances. They don't know women as tragedies. I used to teach a class on Slovak writers in grammar school. I don't know if anyone still does that these days. Do they? I could no longer bring myself to convince anyone that they should know something about Slovak writers. Not that we could justify such a need in the old days either, but back then we didn't need to justify things. Eventually I became so disgusted with Slovak writers that I switched to teaching Russian literature. I wanted to keep away from Slovak misfits. I want to keep far away from them, I really do. Fortunately, writers don't exist anymore. Because to exist is to mean something. But they don't mean anything. We should erase them from our diaries, we should stop phoning them on their name day. They are nobodies. Yet these nobodies haven't even noticed. After November 1989, the Slovak peasants noticed immediately that from that moment on they were nobodies. But the writers didn't notice anything. One of my husbands was a peasant. That's a profession worthy of a man. He was a nobody and never pretended to be anything else. A realist! It's not the socialist realist writer who is a realist but the one who realises that he must stop writing. Just like the peasants and the collective farms. Some of them have become security guards. Like another husband of mine. Many things, many properties need to be guarded these days, protected from vast numbers of thieves, including security guards, against whom other security guards have to be hired. But if you're a sensitive, perceptive, smart person you wake up one night with a bookshelf collapsing on top of you! And you survive even that. Life goes on, alas. But at this point, and no later, you realise that there's something wrong with books, that it's unnatural to cram one's flat and life full of books. Go ahead, help yourself to as many of these fat tomes as you like! Including those with dedications by Slovak writers. We used to think their signatures would be worth something one day. It never happened. Maybe one day the signatures of security guards will be worth something.'

He's fiddling about with an omelette. The other day he ordered Spiš sausages but they were swimming in oil. He quickly had to wash them down with half a bottle of beer so they wouldn't make him sick. But by the evening he had drunk so much beer that he was sick anyway. He wonders about his more sporty colleagues: would they have an omelette for breakfast? Hardly. But perhaps they wouldn't even notice what they were having for breakfast, they suffer strange lapses of memory and concentration, brain dysfunction. That is why they tend to run round and round the track from dawn till dusk because they forget what time in the morning they started running, forget how many laps they're supposed to do each day and so they keep running round and round, and though their strength ebbs away they can't stop for fear that they haven't done enough laps and stopping would be a sign of old age and their impending doom, in which case they might as well join their parents in bed, parents in their seventies who have been bedridden for some time after a stroke, completely helpless and apathetic, dependent on assistance and nappies, their eyes strangely translucent and vacant, and so the runners keep on running, hearts pounding, lungs wheezing, and bellies still flopping about despite daily exercise, and once the runners finally stop running they have nothing better to look forward to than going home to their wives, who are working out on stationary bikes in the bathroom. This is how both husbands and wives exert themselves to the utmost in order to cheat the ageing process and, even more importantly, to cheat one another. The wife wants an attractive body to be sure her husband doesn't leave her, and the husband wants a six-pack to impress his neighbour's wife but, at the same time, he is worried that he might lose his own and their daily rituals, and that along with his wife he might also lose his son, the apple of his eye, who will soon take over from him in the family, because that's what the merry-go-round of life and death is like, the fairground of generations.

Isn't that something to thank God for?

The husband comes home out of breath, sits down, and looks on as his wife acquires more and more wrinkles.

He has no bad thoughts, just looks on.

Then he gets up, takes a bottle of the hard stuff from the fridge and pours himself a drink.

Were wrinkles this important in the old days, too?

Or did everyone in the old days acquire wrinkles at the same time and at the same rate?

Because that's what it looks like, judging by films from the fifties.

On another occasion the husband and his almost sixty-year-old friend go and visit their friend in hospital. On the spur of the moment they decide to race each other to the tenth floor. Their friend's days are numbered. He didn't exercise or compete enough, which is why he has ended up in the ward on the tenth floor. The other two dash towards the staircase, faces screwed up with hatred. As if possessed by the devil. This is just a turn of phrase, because in fact the devil has always been inside them. Only a minute earlier one of them courteously held the door open for the other, now they're furiously bounding up the stairs. One hopes the other will trip and fall down the stairs. The other wishes that the first got out of breath. Or that his lungs would burst. Is such a thing possible even in theory? The first now regrets he agreed to this because he has undergone major surgery and until recently his stomach wound kept opening up spontaneously and the pus had to be regularly pumped out. The other had problems with his blood pressure, a year ago he was so desperate he resorted to applying leeches to his legs, but last week he swam across Lake Šírava and thought a run up to the tenth floor would be child's play, a swift and simple way of humiliating a smug nearly-sixty-year-old who deserved to be taught a lesson.

They pounded, panted, rasped.

Their bright red faces turned green with startling speed.

They reached for the banisters on the never-ending staircase.

'Somewhere around the eighth floor I thought was a goner!' the younger and fitter of the two admitted a week later over a beer. 'That I'd have a heart attack! That something would burst in my brain!'

'I understand,' Andrič nodded although he didn't understand.

Nobody asked if he understood.

'Of course you understand,' growled the nearly-sixty-year-old, 'I don't see what there is not to understand. Sorry to interrupt,' he said affably to the other runner, his rival.

'I thought I'd fucking snuff it there,' the other runner went on, 'but I wasn't going to slow down. Even if I fucking snuffed it out there, I wouldn't have slowed down because this guy here could actually have beaten me. Right, daddy-o?' he said, patting the nearly-sixty-year-old on the back in a prehistoric, Neanderthal show of appreciation. 'I'd rather kick the bucket!'

There was something so profoundly friendly, so protectively beautiful and special in this back-slapping and the subsequent hugging of the older man by this strong, athletically built fellow that it brought tears to Andrič's eyes even as he recalled the scene in the café over breakfast.

Instead of eating, Laura was jotting something down in her diary with an absent expression. Her diary was filled with multicoloured scribbles, post-it notes in a rainbow of colours plastered with phone numbers, reminders and messages. The margins were full of assorted doodles – mostly awe-inspiring emaciated figures, invariably set against an aesthetically pleasing, ingeniously executed and enthrallingly abstract backdrop. Alongside hallucinations, the diary also contained sober facts: the phone number of the hotel manager next to esoteric scribbles, a recipe for crème brûlée as well as the copy of a painting by František Kupka.

So was there anything that Laura actually enjoyed that morning?

As always: only her daughter's joy.

Noble.

Normal.

Terrifying?

'If everything in the world cost only two euros, we would live quite well,' she remarked. 'But today you have to pay two euros for stuff that yesterday cost only ten cents.'

'And to add insult to injury, don't you think the stuff seems to have been split in four?' Andrič enquired. 'Each quarter is being sold as a whole. Or does it have to do with that case of the murdered pregnant maid? Was she quartered?'

On a symbolic level, that case was mainly about the murder of an unborn child. The crime took place in the hotel where Laura worked as a receptionist.

Speaking of Laura's job: she will definitely climb the greasy pole.

She is certainly not satisfied with being a receptionist, she has much more to offer.

It's not a job conmensurate with her skills.

There's no way she won't climb the greasy pole!

She has the motivation, the interest and the intelligence.

Is there anything she doesn't have?

She doesn't have another child.

She could have had another one but didn't in the end.

Andrič brought up an earlier assurance of hers that she didn't want another child although, of course, he understood that it was one thing to talk the talk and another to walk the walk, but eventually he managed to convince her, although it wasn't easy because, when reflecting on being and not-being, some people deliberately don't draw a distinction between the born and the as yet unborn.

And just as they finally reached an agreement, suddenly there was this murder – the symbolic slaying of a mother and her child, with a symbolic emphasis on the child and a symbolic emphasis on the murder.

Andrič must have been around fifteen when he first realised that there was actually no reason for him to have been born in the first place.

Then, as now, the thought upset him: what a wasted opportunity!

'It may still be snowing in St Petersburg today, and yet few people there think the way Raskolnikov did,' said Laura, digressing to her favourite topic.

He gazed at her.

Laura in a fur collar, thirty-six years old.

She always looked beautiful when she talked about books.

She spoke of moments when books have the same effect as drugs, when they are fecund and bring forth other books, when they are strong, healthy and keen to procreate. In these wondrous moments, thanks to the reader's imagination, a book brings forth another book, using the reader as an instrument and turning him into an author in his own right, making the reader write by awakening in him the deceptive illusion that he, too, can do it, though in fact all he can aspire to is to be the shadow of the author of the work that inspired him. But there are times when a shadow writes so obssessively that his writing unwittingly gives birth to something individual and distinctive and the original, inspiring opus suddenly seems to die.

The idea of the death of the old giving birth to the new is well known in alchemy, but what was it doing here?

It was written down in Laura's notebook.

The margin of this particular page was decorated with the shakily drawn image of a foetus.

'Let me tell you an instructive story. It might help you understand my daughter better,' Elvíra began, but he was distracted and stood there sliding his fingertips across the spines of the old tomes, unsure that he wanted to be instructed. Every now and then he would lean closer to a book, taking almost perverted pleasure in inhaling the fragrance of its binding and its yellowing pages. He was suddenly overcome by shame because he realised what Elvíra was thinking: she thought he ought to know more about Laura than he did.

He blushed.

Elvíra noticed his face had turned red and assumed he was a little worse for drink, as usual, otherwise he wouldn't have come over to see her.

She was keen to assist her daughter's inebriated boyfriend.

She might even have made up this instructive story herself: after all, life doesn't offer well-rounded, instructive narratives just like that. Or it has only one to offer per person and, in any case, that person won't be able to understand it until it's too late for them – just as their own story is about to end. In the course of her life this now middle-aged woman must certainly have come by a narrative of this kind and now that its arc was virtually complete, she wanted to share it with Andrič. Nothing strange about that, they had formed a bond: it was obvious from the outset that the two of them were, in a way, companions in misfortune. The causes of their respective misfortune were quite different, moreover, some were contradictory, because what he regarded as misfortune, she had, at some stage in her life, regarded as happiness, whereas what she had experienced as misfortune at some stage in her life, was for him the unattainable happiness he dreamt of, but they were shackled together by the end result: an all-encompassing and earth-shattering misery.

As he leaned forward, inhaling the fragrance of the thick tomes, Andrič was suddenly seized by a fit of coughing and turned to Elvíra exclaiming:

'There are so many texts in this world! Including in this room! And this whole flat! But who's going to read them all? And why should they?'

He somehow clipped a bookcase with his shoulder – it trembled as if there was an earthquake – but managed to catch a falling book in the nick of time and then looked out of the window.

It was night.

In this town at the foot of the mountains it is not advisable to walk the streets at night, let alone go to a pub. The local lads who roam the streets high on drugs are out there hacking each other to pieces, kicking each other's heads in with their Doc Martens, and people blame it all on Americanisation and globalisation and the postmodern situation. But even as early as in 1930s, in Dobroslav Chrobák's story *My friend Jašek*, some youths at a village fête gashed Jašek's face with a broken glass, just like that, for no reason, and then *'they kicked him to within an inch of his life'*.

You have to read the old books to see that there is nothing new under the sun.

He stepped away from the window, gave up on the town at night, smiled by way of goodbye, and made for the door. His hand was already on the door handle when Elvíra began, after all, to tell him her instructive tale.

The waitress brought some more Fernet and suddenly it seemed to him that she, too, resembled Laura. The same hair, the same look of vulnerability in her eyes. This waitress, who seemed to represent a certain kind of woman and a certain kind of female destiny, although she might just as easily have stood for a certain kind of man and a certain kind of male destiny, was living proof that life meant humiliation and real life meant real humiliation. Laura's former husband, the German one, used to humiliate his wife, perhaps on the grounds of inherent national superiority, who knows. But Andrič hated this German specifically, not as a representative of a nation but as a male.

Maleness is a supra-national category.

He didn't even know the German's name.

Knowing that was the last thing he needed!

The name could at any time have given rise to a chain of associations. He may have been called Patrik, and Andrič harboured a long-standing hatred of all Patriks. He knew this was unfair but he couldn't help it. It wasn't that he was intent on exterminating every Patrik, but they were often on his mind and just the other day, when someone in the office introduced himself as Štefan, being completely lost in his confused thoughts, he shook Štefan's hand and said:

'Pleased to meet you, my name is Patrik.'

When it transpired that this wasn't true he had to explain himself at great length but was suddenly at a loss for words as he tried to affix a verbal mesh across the amorphous current of his whirling thoughts, but it turned out that he didn't have enough words and the gauge of the mesh was so wide that all he could do with this equipment was stammer and stutter. The explanation for his bizarre lie or slip of the tongue remained locked inside him like a prisoner with the door of his cell slammed shut. Except that later that night it unexpectedly turned out that on occasion he could be quite articulate: Laura reminded him that a few days ago he had made some remarks that were of great significance.

'And by saying that you ended our relationship,' she informed him.

He was taken aback because he had no recollection of this and he had not been considering ending their relationship. He was usually content with his relationships and never did anything to end them, although it was true that he did even less to foster or develop them: when they existed, they existed and while they existed, they existed the way they did.

'We keep seeing each other even though you have ended our relationship,' said Laura, repeating the information.

Her face didn't look unfriendly.

'Sometimes we sleep together but that doesn't mean that the relationship is still on,' she said calmly, 'we go on days out, we even nearly went on a skiing trip once, as you will recall,' – he didn't – 'and we would even have gone skiing, if you were able to ski – or sledging – we could have gone sledging too, my little girl loves it – but you're not really good at sledging either, as I've noticed – and although our relationship is over, we might give sledging another try, or take a few more walks in the shopping centres.'

The information from Laura unsettled him: where had he found the words to tell her that it was all over?

He could imagine censors banning Thomas Bernhard or Yuri Mamleyev for the words they had used and the context in which they had used them, but he couldn't imagine himself putting anything so important into words. But in all probability there was nothing important at stake here: a few weeks ago he might perhaps have been in a drunken state and waffled on about life, the passage of time, about being happy with the way things were, in this relationship with Laura, particularly the kind of relationship that didn't develop further because he felt no need for things to develop further, he always lived in the given, unmoving moment, although he couldn't deny that at times he also imagined the days or weeks that would follow, but always and only as a part of one undivided whole, like the chewed up gum of an extended and stretched moment, in which there is a woman – here is this woman, as Péter Esterházy would put it –, here is Laura: here you are, he had said to her, maybe a few weeks earlier, I feel good when you're around, only he probably went on to say that he also felt good when Laura didn't happen to be around, he might even have said that he felt better when she wasn't around because he was on his own, and when he was not on his own he was with his mates, different mates on different occasions, he was an individualist with a bunch of individualistic mates, because we are children of our age and we like it, this hedonistic age of ours, he probably said to Laura, for me it's usually enough if one of my mates rings me, he told her, we don't even have to meet, he might phone me and even that's too much, sometimes I prefer it if no one phones, often I'm so scared that they might ring that I've begun turning off my mobile, and once I started to do that I realised that for some time now most of my mates have been keeping theirs turned off for days on end, that's why I can reach them by phone so rarely, even though I don't really try very hard, I'm happy in the knowledge that there they are, in their tower-block dens, we're also children of that earlier age, superficially the exact opposite of our own beloved hedonistic times, although hidden away somewhere in far corners, in secret individualistic nooks and crannies, the cells of our cancerous way of thinking had already begun to proliferate, even if, all things considered, what that age had drummed into us was the value of the community and the family as the bedrock of society and later the Catholic family values blah-blah, but fortunately this drumming automatically produced the opposite effect, because when drumming is applied to untrammelled thought it generally has the opposite effect, and so the values of the family and everything else have been automatically lost, erased, eradicated, nullified, transmogrified, to be replaced by the values of solitude and independence and individual freedom, it may well have been about this that he had waxed lyrical to Laura and was actually pleased to see that Laura had listened to him intently, in the belief that she admired the sharpness of his intellect, the passion with which he imbued everything he said and the way he said it, and how the solitude he used to hate and that had almost driven him insane was transformed into the solitude he yearned for, and how much he appreciated this longed-for solitude in his moments of solitude and how much more he appreciated it when he could not be on his own, and how he felt more and more oppressed and thrown out of kilter when he had to be in someone else's company, and how he had started telling even his mates that he preferred being alone to being with them, he would even tell them at the start of their increasingly rare meetings and get-togethers how many minutes he would like to spend with them and how many minutes, hours and days he would prefer to be alone afterwards, so that he might recall the time spent in their company or in Laura's or in anyone else's, and play back in his mind what had happened, what they had talked about, who had said something interesting and who had just jabbered on as usual, these are the precious moments, he'd say to his mates and this was probably what he also said to Laura, as he fumbled for the few constantly repeated words and word-combinations that made up his too-wide-gauge verbal mesh, in sum, he regarded his stagnating relationship with Laura as proof positive of success and happiness, and from this she had quite logically – though with considerable disappointment, sorrow and bitterness – drawn the conclusion that it was time for her to start looking for a new partner, in fact not a new one but a genuine one, because he was not really a partner, just a passer-by who had been peering over her fence for the last two years.

Laura was competent at all the household chores, earning money, raising a child, repairing the fridge, driving the car, doing the accounts, making plans, doing the cooking, having occasional sex, doing the ironing, having a cigarette on the balcony: she would stand there with her mother and berate her for not giving up smoking even after she had retired, she really ought to know better and indulge herself less, because smoking had recently gone out of fashion while berating people for doing so was now very much in. Elvíra endured these balcony seances with a bland, benevolent and mildly contemptuous smile, since she knew full well where all those cigarettes, medications, illnesses, and advancing age would end.

In the morning she would make herself some coffee and sometimes she also talked to Andrič who would nod sympathetically.

On such days, redolent of coffee and mild cigarette smoke, they got on like a house on fire.

They both drifted along melancholically, without striving for anything.

The only problem was that, unlike her mother and Andrič, Laura was full of energy, brimming with plans. He knew she drew her energy from her young daughter. Not in any vampirical sense: she drew the energy from the sheer fact of her daughter's existence. The child had a future and so it seemed to Laura that she, too, had a future and that was why she was understandably furious with her mother for not applying the same principle: after all, she too, had a daughter, Laura, so she should be happy about that!

But her mother paid no attention to the intergenerational energy-passing baton.

After Laura informed him about the termination of their relationship Andrič gradually began to swell up with a kind of absurd pride about the fact that he, too, was capable of using words, that his words had consequences – and this also applied to statements he couldn't remember at all – but Laura refused to repeat those words of great significance and merely reminded him that he had uttered them in a wine cellar in Spišská Sobota.

So it was in Spišská Sobota that his tongue was loosened.

And why should it not have been there?

Laura is relaxing on a bench in the square.

She has just had an argument at home with her mother who is unbearable because she lives on another planet, sees all sorts of things other people don't see and comes up with theoretical justifications for suicide, as if suicide were salvation. Laura is not prepared to listen to this and even less prepared to expose her little daughter to such talk, since she always listens to everything and immediately asks questions about it.

Laura is sitting on a bench and plans to just sit there for a long time, but now she also has to listen to the monologue of a young mother who is chatting with her friends a little way off.

'You have a pain in your knee? Does it sting like this, do you go jogging on tarmac, by any chance? I have special trainers for tarmac, thirty euros they cost. But even so, yesterday I could barely hobble back from the embankment, why are you limping, Vicky, a friend asked me, he gave me a lift to his place, and we watched ice-hockey. That's what people call it these days. Later that night he called me a taxi because I wouldn't have made it home. So I get out of the taxi near my block of flats and there's this dog. Made me jittery straight away. It's all dark around the supermarket. And there's this chap standing by the stadium with a German shepherd. I'm a bag of nerves with dogs. Its paws suddenly all over me?! I wear headphones, the kind that play music shockingly loud. They block everything out. And suddenly these paws on my back?! What's he doing, I ask its owner. Its paws are all over me. The dog's agitated. So I gave it a smack with my trainer. I walk on and see this bimbo, she's also out with a dog so I go and give that one a good kick too, and it somersaults down the hill. Two birds with one stone. But maybe it's not really about the trainers, maybe it's about heels. That's why I go jogging. Sometimes I take the pushchair too. I watched this video, it had this chick doing squats with her tot. And the baby loved it! You've got to, like, wear the baby out.'

Am I like her? Laura asked herself.

Is it a bad thing if a young mother is unselfconscious, chilled out?

You don't have to be preoccupied with suicide all the time.

Not even twice a week.

Andrič always liked to respond to Laura's references to her mother's references to suicide, even if he had little to say on the subject, and what he did say was more on the level of theory, although in his younger days he hadn't been all that far from practice.

Back then he took a radical approach: if happiness is unattainable, what's the point of living?

Later he realised that it is precisely the certainty of happiness being unattainable that makes it possible to lead a happy and comfortable life.

Way back, Laura reproved young women who were superficial. This was at the time when she was interested in the Russian modernists. Now she listened to the superficial young woman with bated breath, admiring her straightforward and uncomplicated view of the world.

'And Facebook? This Iranian writer messaged me the other day, some kind of perv. 'Coz I'm a blonde, and that's what he fancies, the perv. I went to a ball the other day and afterwards got seventy-four likes. Even though I didn't get to know a single person there! Unbelievable! Loving means suffering, that's the sort of thing they tell me. In German, too, but I don't understand that. Some post it in two languages. Yeah, time to go. Oh, by the way, have you heard about Ukraine? A civil war, apparently. No idea why.'

The beautiful stranger in the café wasn't particularly interested in the other customers and just sat there chewing something.

'Bon appétit,' said Panza, adding that, personally, he had long ago abandoned youthful adventures and as he was pushing sixty the young lady needn't worry, he was just making small talk before dozing off over his glass. This trip to the Slovak mountains was his farewell to youth, maybe to life.

'My sister thinks I've gone on a course,' he said, turning to Andrič for the hundredth time.

'Maybe that's just what you think,' Andrič replied for the hundredth time.

He was eyeing the beautiful stranger and realised that she, too, made him think of Laura. Probably because Laura, too, was still young. He recently had an anonymous phone call from a marketing company, and the woman asked him, among other things, which age group he belonged to.

'I'm an old man,' he said.

'You don't say!' she exclaimed cheerfully. 'How old are you?'

'Forty-seven.'

'Well, I'm fifty-two. Does that make me an old hag in your book?'

'No, it doesn't apply to women,' he lied and realised that Laura always behaved as if she had something else to do. Probably something to do with her daughter. But he felt that she ought to – yes, that's right – she ought to make proper use of her youth.

To ensure she didn't depart with half the cartload still on the cart.

But anyway: what harm was he doing her if, from time time to time he, like her mother, talked to her about the end? After all, he never talked about the end of their relationship, just the ultimate end, and this kind of generalised, apocalyptic musings tend to be vague and meaningless: everyone indulges in them every now and then when they look in the mirror and examine the state of civilisation.

'I hate all this morbid talk!' Laura yelled on such occasions.

She wasn't in the habit of yelling.

In fact, she never yelled.

She sent him text messages about how she hated morbid talk, but her messages sounded like yelling.

Unexpectedly, he experienced a happy moment: he was looking at a fascinating woman.

The woman noticed and lowered her eyes.

Incredible: who still lowers their eyes these days?

They exchanged a few words and eventually she opened up like a flower, to use a cliché.

He was happy, he needed nothing more.

That, and the knowledge that he didn't have to live with her.

At the same time, paradoxically, he still dreamt of living with Laura, parsing the course of their relationship, pinning it onto his wall planner next to the beetles to gain an overview.

That was the wrong approach.

After keeping his performance under continuous review for three months, his boss announced:

'You've been working in this office too long. You no longer make mistakes since your mistakes have long been incorporated into the office guidelines. But what chance is there for younger people? When will they get their opportunity? You have a cushy number here: with your skills and experience you have no trouble meeting your obligations, but let me say it again: what about the younger people? What is to become of the children of party members while you're still hanging on here? You should have evolved! You should have evolved the hell out of this place a long time ago!'

Andrič felt as if a valve had opened up in his body: he would deflate and slither down onto the floor like a winter coat sliding off a hanger.

He was hoping to have a rest at home but couldn't help thinking of Laura.

Now, there's a woman, as Péter Esterházy would have written. She wasn't here, she was at the opposite end of the country. But she did seem to be here.

The woman had often repeated that she loved him. That was a long time ago, in the early days of their relationship.

In the past he may also have been loved by other women, because women are loving, it's in their nature to be loving and they often talk about it, in fact they rarely talk about anything else. Laura, too, wanted him to say that he loved her and she was angry when he refused. But he was of the opinion that one ought to be careful with words. It didn't occur to him that not saying certain words in certain situations was at least as fatal as saying certain other words in certain other situations. Then one day she told him she didn't love him anymore and was going to give someone else a chance. He drew the conclusion that she had never loved him. He was wrong, because he didn't understand women and the flexibility characteristic of their relationships with their partners. Perhaps he was deliberately in error and deliberately failed to understand in order to avoid having to suffer. He and Laura had practically never rowed and in the absence of the noisy, hysterical rows he had been used to in his parental home he couldn't for the life of him understand that after a certain point in time he and Laura were fundamentally at odds with each other.

At night, after his conversation with his manager, he read some short stories by Švantner and afterwards had dreams of blood. When he woke up he realised he needed a new job.

He was burnt out.

But how could he find a job, burnt out as he was?

And what for?

He had a full-time job with himself, he was preoccupied with getting through the basic functions necessary to live.

He got out of bed but went on sleeping.

He was permanently asleep or half asleep – unawakened, unawakened, unawakened – and as he kept turning this phrase over in his head, he gave a sudden start and realised he had fallen asleep on the office toilet.

He heard rustling from the cubicle next to his.

He climbed on the toilet seat.

He stands there peering over the metal wall: a burnt-out Panza is sitting in the other cubicle.

Panza's eyes are bulging, his mouth is gaping open, involuntarily.

A scream is forcing its way out of the new Munch painting slowly, like jelly.

Andrič checks what Panza is looking at.

He is not surprised to discover that Panza is looking at him.

At the annual management meeting everyone pounced on the canapés. Looking at his colleague Sankti, Andrič concluded that he was even more embarrassed to eat in public than he. And he himself was even more embarrassed to eat in public than anyone else, more embarrassed than anyone but Sankti and certainly more than his colleague Vajová, who was actually not embarrassed in the least, even though she had just picked up a slice of ham between her thumb and forefinger and removed it from a canapé onto her plate because she was not allowed to eat ham, and proceeded to chomp away happily at its remains and in fact by this stage in the proceedings Sankti, too, was actually eating quite ravenously, as if he had lost all sense of shame, except that at the same time his face had turned beetroot red and he was trying to eat as if his life depended on it although you could see he didn't want to eat and therefore at least tried to pretend that he wasn't eating at all, maintaining keen eye-contact with the proceedings since they were in a meeting that served the dual purpose of being a meeting and a small-scale celebration, a kind of office party, the year must be coming to an end, Andrič suddenly twigged that the end of the year was coming, where had he been all year, how could this year have gone by so quickly?

He was living in a dream world.

He was floating above the clouds.

In a relationship with Laura.

That's how they put it on Facebook: *in a relationship with*.

In a relationship cloud.

But the cloud thickened into a storm-cloud, it grew dark, and the rumble of thunder could be heard.

The torrential rain gradually turned into sad rain.

So the year was coming to an end.

He bowed his head, chewing quietly, there goes another year, oh well, perhaps they will finally get a bonus although he couldn't recall anything that he or his colleagues had done to deserve a bonus: unless perhaps the fact that another year had gone by without Slovakia's economy collapsing. On the other hand, nobody knew why the economy hadn't collapsed completely and who should get the credit for that. Maybe the bonus will be for at least not having torpedoed the economy, though they couldn't be sure that they hadn't really torpedoed it, since most of the population are torpedoing the economy merely by existing and by the way they are existing, and bureaucrats are no exception.

As he bowed his head, he imagined a nice round figure.

Sankti was aghast with despair, his eyes filled with Sanktiesque understanding and compassion. There was no formal item on the agenda at this moment, everyone was just eating, munching their food in silence, everyone doing their best to keep their mouths hermetically sealed because they were all terrified of making chomping noises, and Andrič came out in a cold sweat when Sankti, his mouth stuffed with ham, bread, egg and grated cheese, suddenly proposed that they all sing some Christmas carols, but at that moment the ice that was beginning to form between Andrič and Sankti broke, as after a few terrifying seconds Andrič realised that Sankti had just cracked a joke to ease the rising tension. Sankti flashed him a conspiratorial smile with his mouth full, to make the point even more clearly and understandably, but at that moment a few pieces of ham, bread, remnants of egg and a lump of grated cheese plopped into his hand, which – like any civilised person would – he had carefully cupped under his mouth, but the debris slipped through his thin fingers and onto his shirt, making Sankti as well as Andrič freeze at this dreadful moment, and they understood that they had lost the battle.

Fortunately, just at that moment the meeting came to an end.

He was excited by the prospect of Laura seeing him naked again.

It might be the last time.

He felt least self-conscious when he was naked, as his exposed intimate parts drew attention away from his general shapelessness, limpness, and flabbiness.

This was how he would have preferred to go to work, too.

The moon was shining in the wintry sky outside the window, the corridor was carpeted, the hotel suite was heated by radiators; Laura was absorbed in a movie about the castrato Farinelli, while he was applying himself to the task of raising her daughter. He didn't object to this task since he considered fatherhood to be in any event primarily a spiritual matter, a way of passing on one's legacy, views, principles, life lessons, warnings.

'She may not be my daughter, but I would like to take care of her,' he had once said to Laura, but even as he had uttered those words they sounded wrong to him.

Is it right for a man to want to take care of someone else's child? The suspicion of pedophilia immediately reared its head.

And how would he take care of her anyway? Laura lived at one end of the country, he at the other. Neither of them had the slightest intention of moving. Circumstances made that impossible. But circumstances could change. Such a change was something they both feared, although it gradually became clear that, in fact, he was the only one who feared it. It could have meant, among other things, that he was satisfied with his life as it was. Or rather: that he had resigned himself to it – one shouldn't mistake resignation for satisfaction.

What Laura feared even more than the possibility of pedophilia on his part, was that at some stage he really might want to move in with her. That he might be prepared to sacrifice his freedom. But why? Just so that he could bewail his lost freedom later? A while back, maybe a year ago, even as recently as six months ago, she had wanted to move in with him, but as she got to know him better, she gradually gave up on the idea. The stuff he'd blurted out in Spišská Sobota was the last straw: Laura wasn't flighty, nevertheless, she decided to cast her net far and wide and someone, some good-looking guy from Central Slovakia, got caught in it. As a precaution, and out of fairness, she informed Andrič of the other guy's existence. She hoped he would accept this new state of affairs in a calm and collected manner because she was convinced that he had never loved her.

'Are you even capable,' she said, probing further, 'of loving anyone?'

Further questions in a similar vein followed.

After that, in the silence that descended, a heavy, grey-black hatred began to swell up inside him, and suddenly they both moved about like bulls in a china shop, even when they were sitting on their respective sides of the untouched bed. Realising that nakedness was no longer an option he started wondering about the guy from Central Slovakia. Laura had told him that this man regarded experience as something enriching, something that opened up new avenues. For Andrič, experience was a source of bitterness, suspicion, mistrust, and anger. Experience was a trap in which he was caught, howling. Worse still, it made him annoyingly vindictive, prepared to wreak vengeance on anyone, without being too selective, liable to lash out at all and sundry. For the guy from Central Slovakia, on the other hand, even the bad things he'd been through were a reason for doing good – he longed to help people precisely because he'd been badly hurt before. Andrič hated him for this attitude even though he'd never met the guy. Hatred engulfed him like an incurable illness.

Everything in this world is an illness, and once it's cured the world will disappear, he told himself, pleased with himself for being so clever.

There was a lamp standing in the corner, emitting a greenish light that gave even someone as vivacious as Laura a slightly corpse-like appearance and lent her daughter's movements the charm of a zombie child.

Therapy is an assault on the very essence of being, he wrote.

'Are you sick?' asked Laura, pressing a hand to his forehead.

'No, I'm just blushing.'

She knew he was often sick.

Being sick is very convenient.

People forgive you a great deal when you're sick.

In the world of sickness logic seems to be suspended, even morons have no reason to be ashamed; indeed, logic itself can turn out to be just another symptom of sickness.

The next morning they went for a walk and thought back on the events of the previous night. Clumps of green grass survived around the manholes at the back of the hotels and restaurants where kitchen staff poured out the slops. Laura walked with her head bowed and lips pursed.

The face of the man selling tickets for the cable car wasn't his own: it was modelled on a Peter Ustinov original.

'I feel like I'm on an alien planet here,' a child's voice in the ticket queue piped up. The young family had come from Mars, but that wasn't enough to attract anyone's attention. In no time at all the family sank into oblivion along with these notes, Andrič wrote, as the wind tried to snatch his notebook, and since he wasn't watching his step he slipped and tumbled into a snowdrift.

Soon afterwards they went to a bar.

A woman in a skiing outfit walked in.

Whenever a woman like this enters a room, she makes the whole place light up and when she leaves, the room goes dark again. But in fact, it depends on who's looking: men will notice this but women won't. Some women might notice that a woman like this has entered, and will immediately suspect their husbands of wanting to cheat on them, but the wives can't see that it was the other woman's entry that lit up the room because they are convinced that it was their own entry that did so.

The truth is, the room is poorly illuminated.

Andrič went to the bathroom, and while he was gone another man took his seat. He had seen the man on the train the previous day, and he had reminded him of the writer Stanislav Rakús. As a matter of fact, he was Rakús's doppelganger.

Except that the man at Laura's table didn't have a goatee.

Actually, he looked quite different from the man on the train.

He was the spitting image of Andrič.

But what does Andrič look like?

At the table that Laura and her daughter shared with the doppelganger, the plot began to thicken. Meanwhile, Andrič was thinking about the guy from Central Slovakia. Apparently he had trained as a masseur. Andrič had always been suspicious of masseurs. The guy from Central Slovakia was trying to improve his chances in our idiosyncratic local labour market, Laura had claimed back at the hotel, but now she seemed surprised that Andrič got talkative all of a sudden, that he gently held her by the elbow while, at the same time, he took out his mobile and started shooting a video of her daughter who had turned boisterous, diving under the table and playing peek-a-boo with a little red doll, a hand puppet that bore an uncanny resemblance to her. The girl was making funny noises as she played, and the other Andrič was guffawing so much that even his mobile shook.

The first Andrič went over to the bar.

'What'll you have?'

The first Andrič replied.

Back at the table Laura lent the doppelganger a book on Dostoevsky by Berdyaev.

Over at the bar Andrič was fuming over a cup of coffee.

The other Andrič was leafing through the Berdyaev.

The child kept peeking from under the table and the room echoed with her laughter.

The stagecoach of the plot trundled on.

There's always one that trundles on.

Andrič observed himself in the mirror above the bar and suddenly thought he was seeing Panza instead of himself. He knew that Panza was a totally humble man, but there was nothing wrong in this, because Panza wasn't humiliated by his humility, rather his humility provided him with the best shield to hide behind. He had a small room behind his humility where he kept all his personal effects in a neat pile, including his shaving kit.

Every single night, Panza lay in bed, the duvet pulled up to his neck, evaluating the events of the previous day and nodding happily.

The duvet made a rustling noise as his stubble slid along the smooth shiny material.

Everything is right and proper, this and that, the evaluator would say, evaluating.

In the morning, as the new day dawned, all he needed to feel happy was to see that life was carrying on even if his personal life had ground to a halt and even if only other people's lives were carrying on, but so what?

He was happy.

He stood on a bridge and looked down at the river flowing below.

How nice that it's flowing!

Let it flow!

Of course, the river could just as well have been a metaphor, but that would have escaped him.

However: was there anyone apart from Panza who would know how and why his duvet made a rustling noise?

Andrič sneezed, having caught a cold in the humid autumn weather, which he continued to carry inside him even though it was midwinter.

The flaws in a text, he noted, sniffling, become apparent only when you read it out loud.

And the flaws in one's life become apparent only once it's been lived to the end.

You delete lines in a text, you come to regret your life.

He admired authors who were capable of reading their work out in public, noting the passages that didn't work, yet still managed to hold the audience spellbound. In theory he, too, knew what face to make and what to say but: how could he do it with the face he had?

What sort of face was it?

It was a face that turned a serious expression into a caricature.

So he combined the caricature of the face with a caricature of the voice and in this way he often managed to pull off the caricature of a performance on stage. But the audience was real and quite reasonably expected a real experience. His disfigured appearance and disfigured utterances were automatically accompanied by disfigured opinions, fractured syntax, disjointed sentences – smoke is still rising from the wreckage – logic has suffered a major head-on collision – the fire brigade in the audience is deploying specialized equipment to rescue fragments of meaning and sense from the smashed-up wreckage of his text.

A single accidentally uttered word – in these situations he only ever uttered words accidentally – was enough to conjure up memories. All of a sudden he would freeze and become catatonic, convinced that he would never be able to move again, that he'd never escape from this accursed place because an accidentally uttered word amidst the wreck of an unfinished sentence would prevent any further verbal means of expression; with his eyes popping he would try to mumble something but couldn't even bring himself to repeat the wretched word that had unleashed the stream of memories, so he would just sit there with bulging eyes, saying nothing, and the audience sat there with bulging eyes, whispering, while he was overwhelmed by the memory inside his head, some detail to do with Laura; or maybe he recalled the curse Diana had put on him one night ten years ago; to cut a long story short, it was something in his memory that had turned toxic, as if his brain had excreted some acid that dissolved memories into the disgusting glop now filling his head, and the glop paralysed him, in extreme cases forcing him to seek God or some other kind of salvation, and the next day the papers would report that this was yet another awkward reading by a very awkward writer.

If he were now in the village of Nová Vieska near Štúrovo, the pub would be filled with smoke like in the good old days. Despite the monstrosities of history, geraniums would be blooming on the windowsills. It would have been a good place for deleting lines and a good time for regrets, all washed down with four shots of Fernet. However, when he realised what his exes probably thought of him, and that included Laura who was also about to turn into an ex, what his subordinates as well as his bosses at work thought of him, what his father thought of him, the father he hadn't seen for eleven years, and even then their encounter had taken place in a courtroom, his face froze and at that moment definitively turned into a caricature.

As he left the bar with Laura and her daughter, he tripped and tumbled into the snow.

The little girl burst out laughing and started running around him in circles.

He adjusted his hat and watched Laura from the snowdrift, wondering: will this woman ever remember me later, when all this has completely crumbled?

Then he looked at her daughter and wondered if this child would ever think of him, if she would remember him making a fool of himself just to humour her, something he had, incidentally, never done before.

Then he looked at the surrounding mountains, houses, villas, and hotels and wondered if he himself would one day, many years from now, ever think of this little town in the Tatra mountains, this place called Starý Smokovec.

And suddenly he wasn't even sure why he would want to remember any of this – maybe to make his own wretched existence seem fulfilled, satisfied in some way – surely not Smokovec? – so that his life didn't consist of just empty, gradual ageing, ebbing away, weakening, vanishing, a departure, so that later he could feel that he too had once cherished illusions, that he too had managed to blurt out something when carried away by his feelings, that he had touched another human body.

As he lay there in the snow he was suddenly frightened that maybe it was not him but Panza who was lying there.

That he himself had disappeared, got lost in a twist of the plot; had he been left behind in Nová Vieska?

He sprang up nimbly from the snowdrift, almost knocking over Laura's surprised daughter, stamped his feet to shake the snow off his trainers – he only ever wore trainers, whether in Starý Smokovec or Nová Vieska – but hang on, wasn't he confusing Nová Vieska with Devínska Nová Ves?

He clutched his head, feeling his thinning hair; his hat was gone.

He never wore a hat.

A rook with ruffled feathers was gazing out to sea.

The wind sprinkled cold droplets of water on the pier.

Andrič revised his attitude to sailors and overseas exploration. He was filled with respect for the courage of seafarers, a respect mingled with the suspicion that rather than being courageous, seafarers were naïve because they are not aware of the dangers posed by the sea.

That makes it a lot easier to be a seafarer. But to be on the safe side, he paid his respects to the statue of a Dutch admiral by the lighthouse and only then walked into a tiny bar in the harbour.

He noticed that live crabs were swarming behind the kitchen door, and spotted the publisher Bagala waiting for him at one of the tables.

This man looks perfectly at home wherever he is, as if he belongs wherever he happens to be.

In a hotel room, like a stranded whale – right where he belongs.

At a bar in a rock club in Haarlem – right where he belongs.

With a joint in an Amsterdam coffee shop – right where he belongs.

With a glass of champagne at a reception at the Crowne Plaza Hotel – right where he belongs.

Dishevelled, unkempt, unshaven, frustrated, on the brink of bankruptcy and madness – but right where he belongs.

Andrič went over to Bagala's table and ten minutes later they were joined by a Dutch translator who ordered a small beer and said:

'The people here in Rotterdam are incredibly dynamic. Everyone wants to achieve something but never does. People in Amsterdam are the same but at least they don't talk about it. That's why it's so peaceful there.'

After a while the two men set out for a walk around the seaside town. Andrič stayed in the pub nursing his espresso. The Dutch people around him kept rattling on about something incomprehensible, which was just as well, at least they didn't bother him. They were probably spouting the same stuff as people everywhere in the world. Unthought through, unedited – that was why he preferred books, their authors had at least made some effort.

He looked around: everything was grubby, used, worn.

Centuries of tradition had worn smooth the surface of the furniture, started attacking the walls and sinking their teeth into the wooden window-frames.

From the window you couldn't see any sailors, only female pensioners and tourists.

He dropped a brown cube into his coffee, but it was probably not sugar.

The beer has borne the name Grolsch since 1615.

If he had been given a glass like this back home, he would have smashed it over the barman's head, but here he didn't want to rock the boat.

The previous day he had sampled frogs' legs in an ancient Chinese restaurant but not even this exquisitely flavoured slime, which he promptly washed down with several glasses of sake, could distract him from memories of Laura.

He would have liked to forget her, not in order to make a new start but so that he wouldn't have to start anything.

His lack of language skills cut him off from the waitress.

She brought the bill, he paid up and in his confusion said goodbye to her in Slovak.

It made no difference what he mumbled, the mumbling served only as a mask.

It was at exactly this time that Laura was already in a relationship with Vincent Blaho. Andrič learned this from Facebook and a girlfriend of Laura's, who was also his friend, later informed him that Blaho was unassuming and decent.

'Kind of ordinary,' she said with an expression that indicated she wasn't going to say any more.

'He's not infatuated with his own ideas the way you are,' she went on. 'He doesn't feel the need to slap them down on paper straight away.'

'I don't feel that need either,' he countered, distancing himself.

When she went to the toilet, he made a note of everything she said.

'You spend your life in cafés,' she said on her return. 'What use would you be to Laura?'

He wrote this down and wanted to start a polemic, even though Michel Foucault despised polemics.

'It is cafés, it is spent, but is it life?' the friend kept needling him.

'Yes, it is,' he replied.

'Yes, it is,' she concurred, 'but only café life. What use was this kind of life to Laura? She needs to provide for her daughter's future! You can't blame her. Child-raising, shelter, clothing, food… She wants her little girl to have everything she needs. Including a father's love. Do you know what Blaho said just a week after they got together? He took Laura out to a decent restaurant, they ordered prawns, there were candles burning on the table, chilled champagne…'

'Laura doesn't even like champagne,' he broke in. 'It's all piffle. And prawns? They're just bloody enormous bugs!'

'What mattered was the atmosphere. I hope you understand that women care about atmosphere. He said he already thought of Laura's little girl as his daughter.'

'But that's sick! He should be reported to the police. Besides – if a prawn gets into a tooth cavity and is washed down with champagne, it leaves a disgusting taste. Blaho has no cavities, you say? Hats off. What kind of guy is he?'

'Unassuming and decent. He listens to Abba. You couldn't manage that.'

'Certainly not.'

'Because he is flexible. He will even dance if need be. He welcomes the opportunity to be flexible. He is happy for a chance to learn to live with another person. I mean, a woman, of course. He longs to have a family.'

'But Laura doesn't listen to Abba!'

'You have no idea what she listens to. The fact is you were never really interested. But that's not the point, in her view.'

'What is the point, then?'

'What matters to her is her daughter's happiness, where they're going to live, and that the three of them should live together like a family. They already are a family! That was never possible with you. She didn't believe you loved her. You never actually uttered those words. Not to mention your relationship with her little girl. That wasn't a relationship. You just tolerated her.'

'It was early days!'

'Early days? It went on for two years! But you didn't get anywhere for two years!' Laura's friend banged her cup down on the table in indignation.

'You're Laura's friend,' he stated, making a note of everything.

When Jack Kerouac was already a serious alcoholic, he usually had beer for breakfast.

Since splitting up with Laura, Andrič had started to have beer for lunch and also for dinner. One morning the health and safety officer came to his office with the boss's secretary.

'Are you willing to take a breathalyser test?' the man asked.

Andrič was willing.

As it happened, that morning he had, exceptionally, not managed to have breakfast: he'd been running a high fever all night, had trouble breathing and by morning his left hand was paralysed and numb.

The health and safety officer and the secretary were out of luck.

'He wasn't over the limit,' they reported to the boss.

'He will be one day,' said the boss.

Translators' Notes

on (mostly Slovak) writers, politicians and works of
literature mentioned in *Big Love*

ANDRIČ – Ivo Andrić, Yugoslav writer (1892–1975)

BAGALA – Koloman Kertész Bagala, Balla's Slovak publisher,
founder of LCA / KKBagala publishers, focusing on contemporary Slovak fiction

ČARNOGURSKÝ – Ján Čarnogurský (1944–), Slovak politician,
prime minister 1991-1992, former dissident and political
prisoner, one of the founders of the Christian Democratic
Movement; currently a practising lawyer.

CHROBÁK – Dobroslav Chrobák (1907–1951), Slovak writer and
literary critic; his collection of short stories, *Kamarát Jašek*
(*Friend Jašek*), appeared in 1937.

Esterházy – Péter Esterházy (1950–2016), Hungarian writer, *Egy nő*
(1995; *She Loves Me*, 1997)

PETRA HŮLOVÁ – (1979–), a prominent Czech novelist and play-
wright with a wide range of published work but regarded as a
feminist polemicist by many critics and social commentators

ŠAŇO MACH – Alexander Mach (1902-1980), Slovak nationalist
politician, who served initially as Propaganda Minister in the
first Slovak Republic before holding the position of Interior
Minister in the government of Tuka from 29 July 1940 until
the state's collapse in 1944.

MEČIAR – Vladimír Mečiar (1942–), Slovak politician, prime minister 1991-1998, oversaw the splitting up of Czechoslovakia.

MOVEMENT FOR A DEMOCRATIC SLOVAKIA, the political party led by Vladimír Mečiar that campaigned for and achieved the division of Czechoslovakia into two separate states in 1993.

POLIAČIK, MP – Martin Poliačik (1980–) Slovak politician and member of Parliament since 2010, former member of SAS (Freedom and Solidarity Party) and currently a member of Progresívne Slovensko (Progressive Slovakia).

RAKÚS – Stanislav Rakús (1940–), Slovak writer

STAVIARSKY – Víťo Staviarsky (1960–), Slovak writer

STOKER – a 2013 Hollywood horror film directed by Park Chan-wook and starring Nicole Kidman, Mia Wasikowska and Matthew Good.

ŠVANTNER – František Švantner (1912–1950), Slovak writer

'UNAWAKENED' ('Neprebudený', 1910) – short story by Martin Kukučín (1860-1927), Slovak writer, leading figure of literary realism.

RECENT TITLES PUBLISHED BY JANTAR

In the Name of the Father *by* BALLA

Translated by Julia and Peter Sherwood

Balla's nameless narrator reflects upon his life filled with failures looking for someone else to blame. He completely fails to notice 'the thing' growing in the cellar. A hilarious satire poking fun at masculinity, the early years of the Slovak state and the author himself.

-- ISBN: 978-0-9933773-5-8

Bellevue *by* IVANA DOBRAKOVOVÁ

Translated by Julia and Peter Sherwood

Blanka takes a summer job at a centre for people with physical disabilities in the French city of Marseille, where her encounter with their severe conditions ends badly. A novel about our inability to escape 'our own private cages', imprisoned by fear, anxiety and mistrust, no less than indifference to others.

-- ISBN: 978-0-9934467-7-1

Hear My Voice *by* DAVID VAUGHAN

International diplomacy has stopped working. A new breed of authoritarian ruler has emerged, contemptuous of the rules of diplomacy and collective security, and willing to lie and bully to build power and influence. Europe's democracies are confused and defensive. It is 1938 and Germany is putting pressure on Czechoslovakia. A young man has arrived in Prague. His job is to interpret and translate, but he finds himself literally lost for words as conflicting versions of the truth fight for the upper hand.

--ISBN: 978-0-9934467-3-3

For further news on new books and events, please visit
www.JantarPublishing.com